Vile Blood 4
Rebirth

Published by Jen Golembiewski

http://jengolembiewski.weebly.com/

Follow me on Twitter: @JenGolembiewski

Like my Facebook Page:
http://www.facebook.com/vilebloodseries

Dedication

For Cassiel, my greatest
blessing.

Part One

Prologue

"Wake up, my child," were the first words she heard as she slowly opened her eyes. Everything was dark and cold. The soft sound of steady thumping echoed in her ears, and soon she felt water trickling down upon her skin. It was moments before she realized that she couldn't breathe, and as she gasped for air she found a mouthful of dirt in its place. She struggled to move her limbs, but it was hard to even budge, and soon she realized that she was buried in earth.

She clawed and kicked at the ground above her, hoping to loosen the dirt that covered her. She felt her fist punch through the ground, and grasp for air on the other side. Her fingers moved freely as she searched blindly for leverage to pull herself out of the cold hard ground. Rain poured down onto her shallow grave, and she began to feel herself able to move without restriction. The earth had become muddy with her sloshing around in it until finally she was able to rise up and take her first breath.

Rain fell upon her face as she wiped the mud from her eyes. She gazed at the sight around her; she was surrounded by darkness except for the stars that twinkled in the sky above her, and the moon whose light shone down upon her.

She slowly rose up and out of her shallow grave, staggering around, and wondering where she was. It was as she neared the edge of a cliff and stared down that she realized that she was on top of a mountain, but she couldn't remember how she had gotten there. In fact she couldn't remember much of anything, except for a strong feeling that there was somewhere she needed to be and she knew exactly how to get there.

Wake up, my child.

Chapter 1

Winston suddenly shot up in bed in a commotion. It took him a moment to realize that he had only been dreaming, and when he did, he took a deep breath and then let out a saddening cry.

A year had gone by since the battle with the Brotherhood, a year since Sarain had died, and in this year, Winston's anguish and loss had not dissipated. He missed her every day, and dreamt of her every time he closed his eyes to sleep. He longed to see her, smell her, and feel her again. Winston had kept the bag of her things that she had once traveled with: an old book, a few clothes that had long since lost her scent, and an old photograph of her and Orran. It was the only image that Winston had of her, but the girl's beauty in the photo had yet to flourish as Sarain's had in life. But even without a recent photo, Winston could not forget Sarain's face. He remembered every line, every curve, and every color of her being.

It was early evening, and Winston's night was just beginning. He was once a man who lived a lavish lifestyle full of excitement and people, but now Winston's days were empty and spent alone. He often stayed in, merely reading or reflecting on the past. When he'd go out, he'd walk the empty streets avoiding people, and sometimes hunting for the beasts that ran off that day of the battle.

As he gazed around his poorly lit, and now poorly furnished house, he realized how much like a prison his home had become. He had destroyed much of his furniture and decorations during multiple fits of anger and loneliness, leaving only the bare essentials for him to live with. Even with the rooms looking so much different now, Winston still could recall the rooms as they were when Sarain was in them; he could still see her sitting on chairs, walking down the hallway, and almost kissing him in his bedroom.

That night Winston felt too full of memories, and knew that he would be unable to spend the next few hours alone in his house; he needed to get out. He left the place immediately, not even caring to lock the door, and began the long trek into town. Shaven had become a much more lifeless small town, with a lot of its supernatural life disappearing and relocating since the demise of Aion and the Brotherhood. Wormwood Alley, where Winston lived, had very few tenants now, and even the alleyway marketplace had shrunk, losing half its vendors.

Winston walked in the cool night air, with stars shining up above, and the moon lighting his path. He walked into town, keeping to the shadows, with his first stop being the local liquor shop. As he walked to his destination, he ignored passersby and vehicles, so much so that it was almost as though they were never there. All life seemed like a blur to Winston, and his world felt gray.

Winston walked into the bright, fluorescent lit liquor store, and shielded his sensitive eyes; it wasn't so much because he was a vil sang that the light bothered him, but because he was so used to sitting around in the dark as of late. He immediately grabbed a bottle of vodka and quickly brought it up to the register to pay. He fidgeted impatiently while the middle-aged male cashier rang him up. The cashier stumbled through the transaction, nervously, as though he was new to the job, and midway through he glanced up at Winston and stated, "Man, you're a pale one." He ignored the comment, and when the register finally popped open, Winston tossed the money at the cashier and walked off without a word.

He wandered down the street, looking for a quiet deserted place to rest his feet. He came upon a park that looked abandoned; swing sets were broken, the slides were rusted, and everything else appeared to be tagged with graffiti. Winston sat down on the one decent bench left in the place. He popped open his bottle and immediately took a long swig; the vodka's dry smoky flavor gushed down his throat, but didn't quench his thirst. He gulped the bottle down, letting droplets of the strong drink escape the corners of his mouth. When the bottle was empty, he brought it down from his lips, but did not wipe his mouth. He sat there, staring out into space, while still clutching onto the empty vodka bottle.

Winston thought about Sarain's lips, and how soft they felt that last night he saw her and kissed her. Her eyes flashed into his mind; her unique and beautiful violet eyes. A tear escaped Winston's eye, and then he heard a crackle come from the sky. Within seconds rain began to pour down, drenching him from head to toe. Winston wasn't sure what was rain and what were tears, but even still, he did not budge. He simply sat there, in a daze, and let the rain continue to pour down on him.

He thought of Sarain and how she would crack a half smile with the corner of her mouth when he would say something amusing. He thought of her crying, scared and lonely but glad to have him come to her rescue. He thought of her holding on to him, desperate to keep him by her side, and kissing him passionately one night so many years ago; images of him touching her, lying next to her, and making love to her, flashed into his head.

Thunder crackled again, but this time with lightening streaking across the sky above. It was in that moment that Winston felt something snap, and he wasn't sure if it was him or the bottle in his hand. Glass dug into his palm, with black blood pouring out the wound. It was a nasty injury, but he didn't feel any pain, instead he felt enraged. He suddenly jumped up and threw the bottle down, smashing it into several tiny shards. Winston cried out in agony, screaming as hard as his body would allow, but the thunder roared along with him, drowning out most of his cries of anguish. He didn't cry over his hand, the wound was nothing to him, he cried for Sarain; losing her was a greater wound than his vil sang body could heal.

He quickly turned his attention to the bench he had been sitting on, and in a moment of torment, smashed his foot through it. He followed that with punching his fists through the old wood and steel, and finally lifting the remains by its base, and tearing the bench out of its cemented ground. Winston sent the bench smashing down and busting into pieces. He screamed again, but this time his voice broke. Winston began sobbing uncontrollably, and collapsed to his knees. He cradled his head in his hands, and cried over his loss. He missed Sarain so much, and knew that he couldn't live without her. He had only spent a short time with Sarain in Shaven, but now everything reminded him of her, and he knew if he was going to have any kind of life again, he had to leave this place.

Winston dragged himself home, with the effects of the vodka already beginning to wear off; just another result of being a vil sang. He trekked through muddy ground and puddles of water. The raining hadn't let up and only further added to Winston's despair. He felt sluggish and tired, and wanted the night to be over. When Winston got home, he glanced around the nearly empty place, and wondered what there was that he really needed to grab to take along with him on his travels. He thought of Sarain's things, but knew taking them with him would defeat the purpose of trying to leave the memories of her behind. Winston thought of his clothes, though so many of them had become torn and tattered from lack of care and hunting, that it was pointless to try and save them. Winston realized that he had nothing that was valuable to him anymore, and this was a depressing thought for him. He let his gaze fall to the ground, and his eyes settled on a stain that lied at his feet. It was the stain of his own blood, from when Kayne ran him through a year ago, his dark blood never fully coming up off the ground.

Winston thought of how he wished he had died that day; he wished that he could be swallowed up into nothingness and cease to be. Or perhaps maybe he could atone for his past sins and find his way to Sarain in heaven; yes, that was the dream, but Winston knew that even if there was a heaven, it would not be a place that would want him.

Winston began to wonder if it was even worth leaving town; could he truly ever forget Sarain? He couldn't forget her before when she had abandoned him of her own free will so many years ago, how could he possibly forget her now? Winston stared down at the stain again, thinking, perhaps it would have been better if he died, and then he thought of how the sun should be coming up in the next couple of hours.

Winston placed his hand on the door handle, his thoughts racing, but with a deep breath, he settled his mind on what to do. He turned the handle, unlatching the door, and as he pulled it open, muddy water came sloshing in. Rain came down so strong and heavy that it was hard to see outside. Winston began to take a step out, but then stopped himself short. He stared out at a figure moving towards him in the rain, unable to tell who or what it was that was coming for him. He raised a hand up to his eyes to shield himself from the windy rain that was blowing up against his face. His eyes began to glow their vibrant blue, as he tried harder to see his visitor.

Winston took a few steps forward into the storm, realizing that he no longer had any fears, and finally he got a good look at what it was coming toward him. A woman stood naked and muddy before him, her hair drenched and matted to her body, dirt caked to her bare feet, and her hands dripping with blood. Her face held an expression of exhaustion, but her eyes looked bewildered. She stood there staring at Winston, with a lost look upon her.

He dropped to his knees, with the muddy ground beginning to give beneath him. Tears fell from Winston's eyes once again that night as he stared up at the figure in front of him.

"You can't be real," Winston muttered, believing he was seeing a ghost. The woman staggered, and suddenly fell to her own knees. "Help me," she cried out, and immediately Winston was on his feet again and moving toward her. He put his arms around the woman, and helped her get back on her tired feet. Her hair clung to her face, and with his hand, Winston pushed back her hair to make sure he had seen what he believed he had saw. A familiar face did indeed stare back at him, but her eyes were unrecognizable.

"Sarain?" Winston said in disbelief. She shivered, holding herself tight, and slowly stared up at him with confusion, and a pair of brown eyes.

Chapter 2

"Sarain, is that you?" Winston asked more clearly, but still she looked at him with uncertainty before finally replying, "I don't know what you're asking me." Winston stared down into her eyes with puzzlement; she looked like Sarain, but her eyes were different. Sarain's eyes were violet, and this woman's were brown. She shivered as though she was cold, staggered like she was fragile, and more importantly, her smell was different; it was not as he remembered her scent being, not like the scent left on her clothes that had slowly faded away. This woman smelled more.....human.

Winston took a step back, and asked the woman a question that was already swimming in his mind, "Do you know who I am?" She stared at him blankly for a long moment, and then answered, "No." Winston felt himself wince, and another tear left his eye. He wasn't sure who this woman was, but she looked a lot like Sarain.

"What are you doing here?" he asked with his voice beginning to get firm. She glanced around, seeming unsure of herself, and muttered, "I don't know.... Something just told me to come here." He continued to stare at her in disbelief, thinking of all the questions he had in his head, and then stated, "Who are you? Where did you come from?"

She shivered, holding herself even more tightly as she struggled to answer through chattering teeth, "I woke up on top of a mountain… I climbed down jagged, sharp rocks, and I've been walking for miles…to get here." "But why, who are you?" Winston pleaded with her. "I don't know," the woman cried.

Finally, she staggered once more and then collapsed again. Winston quickly went over and swooped up the nude and muddy Sarain look-a-like. She had passed out from exhaustion, and he could feel that her skin was much colder than a human's should be, but as he stared down at her, he saw the blueness in her lips and nails, and realized that she must have been suffering from hyperthermia. He quickly carried her into his house, and took her into the bedroom, where he placed her on the bed, and immediately wrapped her up in every blanket that he could find. His own body could do nothing to warm hers, so Winston prayed that the blankets would provide her with enough warmth.

He stared down at the unconscious woman, still in awe over how much she resembled Sarain; in fact, with her eyes closed he was almost certain it was his departed love, but knowing what hid beneath her eyelids, Winston knew that she couldn't be Sarain. Besides, Sarain had died, and turned to ash, taking her father, Aion, along with her. Winston didn't know of any way someone could ever come back from the dead, or even a vil sang becoming human again; both things were impossible, even in the wondrous hidden world he dwelled in.

But still, a little light of hope flickered in Winston as he thought, "If anyone could figure out how to come back from the dead, surely it would be the uniquely born half-breed spawn of an ancient." But he wondered still, that if this was indeed Sarain, why did she not know him? Why did she have no memory at all?

Who was she?

She stood there, looking up at a door atop a short staircase. She stood before a brownstone home in a city. She wasn't sure why, but something felt familiar about the place, and she felt herself wanting to go inside. She took each step carefully, and reached for the doorknob. She turned it slowly and pushed the door open with it groaning softly. She glanced at the doorframe, curiously, feeling as though there was something about it that she should know, but she didn't.

She stepped inside the nicely furnished home, greeted by the smell of food baking in the oven. The sound of a television playing echoed from nearby, and she decided to follow the sound. She walked into a living room, where she saw the television on what looked to be an action movie; there was a man and a woman fighting with swords and they were fighting an army of people, but something looked off about the people. She tried to focus on the movie, but the screen appeared to get blurrier the more she tried to watch. Finally the television shut off, and she realized that she was not alone in the room.

She looked over to see a man sitting on the couch, holding the TV remote. He was a handsome man with tanned skin and closely cropped brown hair. He smiled at her lovingly, and patted the empty room on the couch next to him, motioning for her to join him. She cautiously approached the man, though a feeling inside her told her that he could be trusted. She sat down next to him, and he immediately took her by the hand, and it was in that instant that she realized that she was wearing a wedding ring, and that this man also wore a wedding band.

"Did you have a good day at work, Hun?" he asked her, but before she could answer, he added, "I got called in to patrol tonight, I'm filling in for a buddy's shift, so I'll be late." She glanced and saw a police badge on the coffee table, and she turned and gazed up at the man. He stared down at her with his brown eyes, but before another word could be said, someone else walked into the room. "Mom!" a voice called out, and she immediately turned to see a boy standing in front of her. The boy appeared to be eleven or twelve, and also appeared to be referring to her, but he looked too dark to be their son, at least biologically.

"Mom, can I have some money to go to the arcade?" the boy asked. "Hey, what's wrong with your games upstairs?" the man questioned. "Nothing, I just want to meet the guys," the boy replied. She turned and glanced at the man with confusion and he said, "It's up to you." She turned back to the boy and softly answered, "Sure." The boy smiled, and gave her a hug. The hug caught her off guard, but something felt oddly fulfilling about it. She wrapped her arms around the boy, and gently patted him on the back. Then she heard herself saying, "I missed you," to him, as a tear fell from her eye.

After a moment, the boy pulled away with a smile, and went off to raid her purse, leaving her alone with her apparent husband, again. She looked up at him once more, and still he continued to gaze upon her lovingly. "Well, it looks like it's going to be just the two of us for the next couple of hours, what did you want to do?" he said with a smile.

She felt herself blush, but before she could speak, he leaned in as though to kiss her, but then stopped short with his lips just inches away from hers, and he whispered, "I'll always love you...... And I wish you could stay....... But this is not your life..... You have to go."

She stared up at him with pleading eyes, but it was of no use; he was right, and she was needed elsewhere.

Chapter 3

She opened her eyes, and the first thing she realized was that her hands and feet felt sore. She gazed down to see that her hands were bandaged up, and then she noticed that she was now wearing clothing. A blanket covered her as well, and she had been tucked into bed like a child. She appeared to be cleaned of the blood and dirt that had caked her body earlier, but she was alone in the bedroom that she laid in now.

She rolled onto her side, and waited quietly for a moment, contemplating whether or not to leave the bed. She wasn't sure where she was, but she assumed that it had been the man she had met earlier that had taken care of her.

She gazed around the room to see that it was mostly bare of decorations; there was a dresser that appeared to have once held a mirror, but the glass was now missing, and the backing looked as though the mirror had been smashed out. Slowly, she slid out of bed, and crept to the door, not knowing what to expect on the other side of it. She tried to listen for sounds of movement, but her ears were not strong enough to hear very far. Finally she decided to take the risk, and opened the door. She peered out to see a small empty hallway, and while taking a deep breath, she stepped out and walked down the hallway and into the den.

There, the blond man she had met earlier laid on an old beat up looking couch. His eyes were closed, and he appeared to be sleeping. She glanced around the room, noticing that there were no windows or clocks that she could see, and she wondered what time it was. She crept to the door, and slowly cracked it open, hoping not to wake the sleeping man, and wanting to see what time of day it appeared to be.

Light came bursting in, gently warming her skin, and it looked to be mid-morning. Suddenly she felt the door slip from her fingers and slam shut, causing her to turn around to see the blond man standing in front of her, a stern expression on his now reddish sunburned looking face. This startled her, and she noticed that smoke was coming off the man's skin.

"The sunlight burned you," she quickly commented with surprise, but after taking a moment to think things over, she realized that she wasn't really scared by the occurrence, just a little shocked. But deep down, she felt as though she should have known better, and then she said, "I'm sorry." He looked a little surprised by her apology, and even more so by the fact that she didn't appear to be scared of him.

"It's okay, you didn't know," he replied and moved back to the couch. She followed him, sitting down on the other end, and an awkward silence proceeded to fall upon them. She gazed down at the long large shirt she was wearing, and she heard him say, "I hope you don't mind that I cleaned and dressed you. I'm sorry that I did this while you were unconscious, but the color had finally come back to your skin, and I didn't want your wounds getting infected."

"I have a feeling that that is okay with me," she answered sounding a little confused. He gazed over at her, looking her in her eyes to the point that it made her feel a little uncomfortable, before finally asking, "You really don't remember anything about yourself?" "No," she replied. "Because you look a lot like someone I used to know," he remarked, and then added, "Except for your eye color." She thought this over, understanding now why he kept staring at her, and then she asked, "What happened to this friend of yours?" He hesitated for a second, before answering, "She died." She closed her eyes to think, and asked, "What was her name?" "Sarain," he replied. She opened her eyes, and said, "Then that's what I want you to call me, at least until I remember who I am."

He sighed, almost sadly, before agreeing, "Okay…. Sarain…. You can call me Winston."

A few hours went by, all filled with quiet awkwardness. Sarain's stomach at one point started growling so loudly that Winston noticed, and said that he would get her food once it grew dark out. Sarain spent the remainder of the time in the bedroom, until Winston left. There was something about him that made Sarain nervous, and because of this she didn't know how to act around him.

She gazed down at the t-shirt she had been wearing, and realized that she felt exposed with most of her legs showing, and no undergarments on. She searched around the room for suitable clothing, but most of Winston's clothes were too big for her. Then Sarain noticed a backpack with a dark sleeve hanging out of it. She unzipped the backpack and pulled out a black long sleeved shirt, and a pair of black pants; all the clothing inside appeared to be black, and all in her size. She took off the t-shirt she had been wearing, throwing it on the floor, and slipped into the form fitting, spandex like, black clothing. Something about the clothes felt freeing; they allowed her to move without restraint, but still covered the majority of her skin, and something about that gave her a strange sense of security.

Happy with her new attire, Sarain headed into the living room to wait for Winston to return, and as she headed for the sofa, she noticed a dark stain on the ground that she hadn't given much attention to before. She stared at it curiously, wondering what it was, and she bent down and crouched to examine it closer. She lowered her hand to the ground, and let her fingers graze the surface of the floor where the stain lay. And for a second she envisioned the room filled with beasts, but the image only lasted briefly in her mind, and merely left her confused and wondering if she had just had some kind of strange nightmare.

Suddenly the door creaked open, and Sarain spun around to see Winston standing in the doorway with a couple bags of groceries in his arms. His first thought was; why was she staring at his bloodstain so strangely? And then he noticed what she was wearing; she had found "her" clothes. Seeing her wearing those clothes sent a tinge to his un-beating heart, making him feel both disturbed and overjoyed to see such a familiar looking site, but all the while a voice in the back of his head said that this woman may not be his love, Sarain.

Sarain gazed over at Winston, reading the expression on his face, and she remarked, "I hope you don't mind me wearing this; it was the only thing I felt comfortable in." He stared at her for a moment then nodded his head slowly, and replied, "It's alright... It looks good on you." Suddenly Sarain felt herself blush, and Winston immediately noticed, and a small smile spread across his own face. Then Sarain's stomach growled and she remembered that she was hungry. Winston placed the groceries on his table, with Sarain soon by his side, quickly looking through the food. She pulled out a jar of pickles, placed her bandaged hand on the lid, and tried to open it. She grunted, and Winston noticed that she was straining to get the jar open, but failed to do so. He couldn't believe what he was seeing; the Sarain he knew was powerful, and able to punch her fists through the stone-like hide of a demon, while this Sarain couldn't open a simple jar. Given, her hands were bandaged, but the old Sarain had been able to do much more with much worse wounds.

Winston took the jar from her, and quickly unscrewed the cap, and handed the lidless jar back to her. She thanked him bashfully, and soon started eating the pickles inside. She made her way through the other groceries as well, sampling a little bit of everything. Sarain ate as though she had not eaten in ages, surprising

Winston once again; his Sarain scarcely ate, but this one ate as though she had been starved.

When she was done, she accidentally let a little burp slip out, and her face turned red with embarrassment. She sighed looking at the door, and she turned to Winston and asked, "Do you mind if I go outside?" "You're free to come and go as you please," he stated, and then added, "As long as you don't burn me with sunlight again." Sarain blushed once more, and headed for the door, but as she took her first step out into the cool night air, she turned to Winston and said, "Will you come out with me? I don't know what's out there, and I have a feeling that I'm safer with you."

Now it was Winston who felt himself blush. He stared back at this Sarain, seeing vulnerability in her eyes, and then he remembered the night that Sarain asked him not to leave so many years ago; the night that they had made love. And he realized that the look in this girl's eyes was the same look Sarain had given him that night, a look of helplessness, and wanting him by her side.

Winston then understood that he wanted to protect this Sarain just as he did the one before, whether they were truly one in the same or not, and he stepped outside into the darkness behind her.

Chapter 4

Sarain took a deep breath, letting the cool night air fill her lungs. The sky was surprisingly cloudless for having rained so heavily the night before, and stars filled the sky, twinkling with beauty.

"Being out here feels so right," she muttered softly. Winston gazed at the energetic girl, not used to seeing a happy Sarain, and still wondering if this was the same person he knew before, when he stated, "Perhaps you're remembering your old self." "I wish I could, I feel so lost not knowing who I am," she responded.

Even with her inability to remember, Winston noticed that Sarain was able to smile, and then a thought occurred to him; perhaps this was the same Sarain he knew and loved, and that she only seemed different because all the years of hunting and living alone were wiped from her mind. All the dark memories and agonizing losses were gone, leaving the purer spirit and innocence, which she had lost so long ago. Though he still couldn't understand why she now seemed so human, Winston thought it best not to question the miracle that had happened, and be grateful that Sarain was once again back in his life.

"What did you want to do?" he asked her. "I think I just want to walk... That is, if you don't mind walking with me," Sarain answered. "Not at all," he replied, keeping pace with her. Sarain took the lead, walking into the desolate desert that was Wormwood Alley, with a spring in her step. She seemed happy and almost child-like as she glanced around at everything, looking up at the stars, and picking up rocks and throwing them as they walked along. Winston steadily followed after her, but felt as though he was simply there as a voyeur. Sarain appeared quite happy in her own world, hardly acknowledging Winston's presence, until finally she stopped in her tracks and glanced back at him with a huge grin on her face. This was a look Winston had never seen her make before; a look that made him doubt that she was the same Sarain he knew and loved; but still, her innocence and happiness seemed so unique and appealing to him, that he was curious to what else this new Sarain had to show him.

It was then that Winston recognized their surroundings and realized what it was that had made Sarain so excited. He gazed at her as she stared up into a darkened stairwell, and before he could stop her, she jumped up into the darkness, and hurried up the staircase. Winston quickly followed her, hoping to reach her before she reached the top of the stairs, and as he neared the top he saw her waiting there for him, gazing out at the vendors and shoppers that moved outside.

"Look at all the people," she muttered. "I know," Winston stated, "It's a market place." Sarain smiled with excitement, and then said, "I want to go there!" And she quickly jumped out through the false brick wall and into the marketplace.

Panic ran through Winston as he immediately followed after Sarain. He didn't know how to explain to her that if the wrong people recognized her, she could be in grave danger. When Winston reached Sarain, she was standing at a booth where a bunch of random and harmless looking items were spread across a table. He noticed her staring intently down at an old metal hand mirror, and he wondered what thoughts were running through her mind. He saw Sarain slowly pick up the mirror and bring it up to her face, gazing intensely at her own reflection. The mirror didn't appear to be anything special, and Winston didn't sense any enchantment to it, but still he watched Sarain who was enamored with the item. Then Winston recalled how the old Sarain had hated mirrors, and even once witnessed himself, a dark aura that had tarnished her reflection. He never fully understood what it was that Sarain had seen in mirrors, but as he watched the new Sarain stare at herself, he heard himself asking, "What do you see?"

"Just me," she said after a moment. Winston found her answer a little odd so he asked, "Then why do you seem so captivated by that mirror?" "… I don't know," she responded, "I guess I'm just trying to see if I recognize myself…" Sarain put down the mirror, and turned to Winston and asked, "Can we continue to look around?" He glanced around at the few people, checking to see if anyone was watching them before settling with the answer, "Sure."

As they walked away, Winston noticed Sarain's gaze going back to the mirror for a moment, and he realized what it was about her expression that he couldn't figure out before; she appeared to be waiting for the mirror to do something, almost like she truly expected for something to happen. And there was a hint of fear in her eyes as they walked away from the item.

Over the next hour, they looked at enchanted daggers, vials filled with potions, cloth sworn to be indestructible, strange animals for sale that were thought to be extinct, and exotic dried meats that Winston would not let Sarain try. They were moving on to yet another vendor when something caught Winston's attention from the corner of his eye; not too far away stood a tall man who didn't look particularly strange except for the fact that his eyes had a gold-ish tinge and were fixated on Sarain. His stare on her was intense and he had a strange sort of smile upon his face that made Winston uneasy, and he began to detest the man. Winston tried to ignore him as he stayed close to Sarain while she obliviously explored the items of another booth. Winston tried to determine what the man was; he wondered if he was a vil sang, though the man wasn't really all that pale, he did though stand about a half a foot taller than Winston who himself was tall, standing at six feet two inches. The man looked to be in his forties with short dark hair that looked a bit unkempt. Other than his height, the man's stature didn't seem to be that much more than average, but his golden eyes were what made Winston uneasy, because he knew that eyes of that color were usually kept by someone with heavily demonic blood. The man didn't seem to have any other demonic features besides his eyes, but they were enough to make Winston worry because the only people that he had ever known to have that kind of unique eye color were Sarain and her father, Aion.

Suddenly Winston felt a tap on his shoulder that nearly made him flinch as it broke his focus. He turned to Sarain who held a silver bracelet in her hand as she asked, "Can I get this?" Winston nodded yes and handed her some money. When his eyes went to look for the strange man again, Winston found that the man had vanished; he quickly scanned the alleyway, but could not find the man again. He didn't know if he should be relieved or concerned by the man's disappearance, but after Sarain finished paying for the bracelet, Winston took her by the hand and said, "We should really be getting back." A look of disappointment reflected in her eyes, but she replied, "Okay," and followed Winston back down the alleyway.

As they neared the false wall exit of the alley, Winston began to feel at ease until a couple moved across his path and after they left his view, revealed that the golden eyed man was waiting at the exit, watching him and Sarain. The man then approached Winston who felt tense from fear that Sarain had been recognized, and the man stared down at him with his face expressionless. Winston's grip tightened on Sarain's hand who suddenly realized that something was wrong and she looked to him for guidance.

The man began to stare at Sarain again as he finally spoke, "She really is something special," he then turned to Winston and asked, "How much for her?" Winston felt appalled as he held on to Sarain firmly, staring up at the man and replying, "She's not for sale."

"Surely there must be something we can agree upon, just name your price," the man insisted. "There's no amount of money you could give me to make me to part with her," Winston bellowed. The man suddenly looked intrigued, and he then responded, "Well if it's not about money, then how about a trade; her, for a virgin girl, or perhaps two?" "No deal," Winston stated sternly, "Like I said before, she's not for sale!" The man suddenly looked disappointed, but instead of getting forceful or angry, to Winston's surprise, he simply reply, "What a shame, well it was worth a try." He then stepped out of their way and let Winston and Sarain walk on by, but as they were leaving, they heard the man call out, "If you ever change your mind, come find me here."

They hurried down the stairwell with Winston's grip still tight on Sarain's hand, and once they were out and headed back home, Winston continuously glanced behind them to make sure they weren't being followed. After about a mile, Winston finally slowed his pace when he realized that Sarain was having trouble keeping up, so he stopped for a minute to let her catch her breath. This was another realization how the new Sarain was different from the old, and Winston found him reminding himself that this Sarain was human and could not do all the things that the old one could.

Suddenly Winston realized that he still held Sarain's bandaged hand firmly, and he quickly let it go and said, "Sorry if I hurt your hand, I just wanted to get out of there as quickly as possible." "Ya I noticed," Sarain replied in such a manner that it reminded him of the old Sarain, but then her features softened and she spoke, "It's okay, I understand; that man scared me too."

She then reached for Winston's hand again and placed her own inside it as she remarked, "Besides, my hands don't really hurt anymore." This was meant to make Winston feel better, but instead it left him feeling puzzled; he had wrapped the bandages on her hands just the day before, and the cuts had looked deep and should have taken at least a week to heal. He knew the old Sarain healed fast, and perhaps if it was her violet eyes staring upon him he wouldn't have thought much of the comment, but the brown-eyed Sarain should not have that kind of healing. The curiosity in him brought Sarain's hand up to his face, and he began to unravel her bandage, and as the dried bloodstained cloth unwrapped, Winston nearly gasped as his eyes settled upon the pristine white skin that lay underneath. There wasn't even so much as a scar from her wounds, and while Winston held on to the calm and un-amazed Sarain, he felt himself almost begin to panic.

And then suddenly Winston heard the words of the man from earlier, echoing in his head; "She really is something special." And he wondered if the man knew something about her that he didn't.

Chapter 5

They reached the house without much else said. Sarain had a look upon her face as though she was worried about what Winston was thinking; she felt as though he was mad at her and she couldn't figure out why. Winston tried to act as though nothing was wrong, but his ability to play it cool had been dampened by the fact that he had hardly interacted with people in the past year. And with dawn soon approaching the two went to sleep in their separate rooms without another word.

It took Winston awhile to fall asleep as he lay on his worn-out couch; he spent a couple of hours thinking about Sarain and trying to make sense of the last twenty-four hours, and her sudden existence again. He couldn't think of a reason why or how she could be back short of making a deal with the devil, but even if such a thing were possible he surely doubted that she would have come back with such an innocent and pure demeanor. This Sarain stared at him with the eyes of a child and little of her personality reminded him of the Sarain he knew.

Eventually sleep found Winston, and he began to dream of the old Sarain; her violet eyes staring up at him, and her pale skin brushing against his. He dreamt of her moist, soft lips kissing him, and her hands caressing his back as her legs wrapped around him. He dreamt of their stomachs moving against one another as their bodies entwined, and just as he began to feel the joy of such a dream, he heard her call out his name. Winston didn't think much of it, since such a thing was normal during this kind of act, but then he heard her crying out his name again, this time it came out as more of a scream and sounded full of fear.

Suddenly Winston found himself startled out of his dream. He shot up and off the couch, quick to his feet, and began rushing down the hallway towards the bedroom where he could still hear Sarain calling out, "Winston!" He swung open the door to see Sarain sitting up in bed, covered in sweat, and her dark eyes looking bewildered. Her gaze quickly fixated on him, and she began to incoherently mutter, "They killed them! They killed them all!" "Who did?" Winston instinctively asked. "The monsters! They killed families!" she cried out. Winston then sat down on the edge of the bed next to Sarain as he remarked, "It was just a dream, there's nothing to be afraid of."

Suddenly Sarain's hand shot out and she grabbed Winston by the wrist, as she abruptly stated, "I have to kill them before they kill me!" He stared down into her eyes for moment; there was a strange look inside them, a look that he had only seen in the old Sarain's eyes once, when she had thrown a knife at his head back when they were still enemies. In a matter of seconds, Sarain's brown eyes softened, and the innocence was restored to her gaze, and then she looked up at Winston with remorse.

"A dream…" she mumbled, "You're right… That's all it was." The remark seemed almost eerie to Winston as he stared down at Sarain, and wondered if it had indeed only been a dream. She then stared back up at him, and a soft smile spread across her lips as she said, "You're always saving me." Winston immediately had a flash of a drunken Sarain saying something similar here on this same bed, and the memory made him feel uneasy. The new Sarain then lifted her hand to Winston's cheek, and she gently caressed it, and stated, "I'm glad you found me." His chest began to tighten as he realized that Sarain had said those exact words to him before, and then he saw her begin to lean in towards him with her eyes closing and her soft lips starting to pucker.

Winston suddenly pulled back, and muttered, "No." And a look of shock came over Sarain. He quickly stood up and stuttered, "Y-you need your sleep." A hurt look was in Sarain's eyes as Winston left the room, but he couldn't help feeling the overwhelming sense of shame at the thought of taking advantage of this Sarain as a form of trying to be close to the one he knew. He still wasn't sure if the women were one in the same, but what he did know was that he wasn't going to be getting much sleep anytime soon.

A few hours had gone by when a bored and rested Sarain came tip toeing down the hallway. As she reached the living room, she saw that Winston was once again sound asleep, and she continued to quietly move for the door. This time she was careful to only crack the door open enough so that she could squeeze through, and lucky for her, the sun was already in the position of afternoon and casting its light away from the door.

Sarain squeezed out of the house and gently closed the door behind her, then proceeded to walk in the direction of where she believed the town to be. As she walked, she stole quick glances at the sun; its warmth and brightness for some reason seemed rather odd to her, but at the same time it felt comforting in a way that she couldn't understand. She hiked along the desert landscape until she reached the stairwell that led up to the marketplace. She then thought of the man that had wanted to buy her the night before; surely he'd be gone by now, and with the light of the sun on her back, she felt as though she did not have to worry about his presence being there.

Sarain proceeded up the stairs and then out into the marketplace. A lot of the vendors had closed up shop, but a few still remained opened, those whose items seemed a little more normal. Sarain didn't seem concerned with the vendors though, she was much more curious on what lied on the other end of the alley. She steadily paced through the marketplace, until she reached the opening that led to the streets. When she stepped out into the town of Shaven, she gave a quick glance behind her to make sure she wasn't being followed, only to be amazed by the fact that the alleyway behind her looked narrow, tiny, and empty. This must have been another optical illusion, set up to hide the real truth of the marketplace.

Sarain then proceeded down the streets of the small town, wanting to see what all it had to offer. The stores were all mom and pop stores, looking old and rundown. The park was abandoned of children, graffitied, and in shambles. Homes that were once ideal for families were now vacant and trashed. The whole town looked as though it had been hit with a wave of bad luck and poverty. Even the trees and ground looked dried up and dying and Sarain wondered what could have caused such desolation, being unaware that Shaven had once been a mystical town that now had been mostly abandoned by its supernatural entities.

As she walked the town, almost everything lacked of life, and she was about to head back when she turned the corner and saw a tall cathedral looming before her. It was built with gray bricks, and stained glass hung in the windows. It held a large brass bell in its tower, and was surrounded by tall black iron fencing. It was a stunning display of gothic beauty, complete with a stone angel sculpture that held a bronze sword in his hand, standing before its doors. Sarain stared up at the large iron cross that hung above the churches double doors, and then her eyes went to the sign that read: Church of the Warrior; Sanctuary to any soul willing to fight the good fight.

She stood there for a moment, simply staring at the structure, and began to feel as though the building was inviting her in. Sarain opened the unlocked iron gate and stepped onto the hallow ground. She proceeded up the stone steps to the double doors, only stopping for a moment to admire the angel statue, which had the name Michael engraved on its base.

When she reached for one of the double doors, she found that it was quite heavy and strained as she pulled it open, echoing out a loud groan as it moved. Sarain stepped inside and onto the mosaic tile that ran throughout the floor of the chapel. The building had a strong scent of incense and candles burning, and rows of wooden pews lined before her. At the other end of the chapel stood an altar surrounded by tall candles, and on the wall hung a large hand-carved crucifix.

Sarain walked down the center aisle of the empty chapel, and stopped once she stood before the altar where a bible and a small bundle of sage laid. And with a strange urge, Sarain extended her hand until her fingertips touched the front of the bible, as if unsure what it might do. She traced the golden embossment of a cross on the cover, and still nothing happened. She didn't know what she expected; just that something inside her led her to wonder if she would be allowed to touch such an object.

Suddenly Sarain heard a creak that caused her to pull her hand away from the bible and turn toward the direction where the sound had come. In the doorway of a side door that led to another room, stood a man approximately in his mid-twenties. He was pale and slender and wearing a priest's frock. He had brown hair and gentle gray eyes, and he spoke softly as he asked, "Can I help you?"

Sarain took a step away from the altar as she replied, "Sorry, I was just curious about the building, I didn't mean to trespass," and she turned to leave when the man said, "It's okay, you've committed no sin; we welcome all who are seeking guidance." Sarain stopped and turned around to face the priest as she relayed, "I'm not looking for guidance." "Still, you walked through our doors, I give it that a part of you must be feeling lost," the young priest remarked. Sarain then felt a wave of fascination come over her and she suddenly said, "Actually, I am suffering from amnesia." "Are you seeking care for this?" the man immediately spoke with concern. "Well, I'm staying with someone that I consider a friend," she replied. "And do you trust this friend with your care?" he asked. "I do," Sarain answered. "Then perhaps in time your memories will return when you are ready," he stated, and then added, "Though if you are ever in need of help or guidance, you may return here at any time."

"Thank you," Sarain replied, "I just might do that." She then smiled at the priest and took a few steps to exit the chapel when the young priest called out, "I'm Father David, by the way." Sarain then stopped for a moment, long enough to glance back and say, "I'm called Sarain," and then she turned around left the chapel.

Sarain began her long trek home, it had yet to become dark, but dusk was rapidly approaching. She made her way through the mostly empty streets, only passing a few kids playing with a kickball in the traffic-free road. Sarain stopped and glanced at the boys for a moment, they looked to be around nine or ten years old, and there were three of them. They ran up and down the street kicking the ball back and forth to one another, and as she watched the kids at play, Sarain found herself sighing without really knowing why. Something about the boys made her feel sad, and she thought about the dream she had had the other day, where she had a son, a family. And suddenly Sarain came to the notion that she believed that she didn't have a family; given, in her current condition, she wouldn't remember if she truly had one or not, but something at the core of her felt as though she lacked that particular fulfillment.

Sarain sighed again, and began to walk away from the kids at play when she noticed something odd; off in the distance, partially hidden in the shadows of a large willow tree, was what appeared to be the figure of a man, standing very still and seemingly staring out at her. Given the man was much too far away for Sarain to get a good look at him, but she could almost swear on the fact that he appeared to be watching her. She began to feel a bit uncomfortable as she turned and walked away, continuing to head back to Winston's. After a moment of walking, she glanced over her shoulder to see that the figure was gone.

Sarain eventually made her way back to the alleyway that housed the magically hidden marketplace, and as she stepped into the now busier bazaar, passing newly opened venders, she felt as though a pair of eyes were once again settled upon her. Her eyes glanced back and forth, but made contact with no one. Sarain continued to walk towards the end of the alley, and as she readied herself to step through the faux brick wall, she took one last glance behind her. For a moment she could have sworn she saw glints of yellow, like a pair of eyes, but upon a better look, saw nothing or no one that could have been responsible for such a thing.

Perhaps it was just the sun's light reflecting off some merchandise; Sarain decided to shrug it away and finish heading on home, and then she thought of how Winston was likely waiting for her, and a smile began to spread across her face.

She stepped through the wall now oblivious to anything other than her own thoughts, unconcerned by the possibilities that someone or something might be following her.

After all, what would anyone want with her?

Chapter 6

Winston opened his eyes. He had a feeling that he had overslept, and then he remembered the events of the night before; he had evaded a kiss from the amnesic Sarain. Winston groaned as he got up, and he wondered if there were going to be any repercussions from Sarain for having done what he did, or didn't do. The old Sarain would certainly have been hurt, perhaps even angry, if Winston had done such a thing to her, but with this new Sarain, he was unsure.

Winston stood up, and realizing that it had to be near dusk, gave a quick glance around the room. Where was Sarain? He wondered if she could be in the bedroom still, perhaps avoiding him. He walked down the hallway, and right away noticed that the bedroom door was open. He peered inside, and, upon reaching the door, found the room empty.

A feeling of panic came over Winston, and then he thought to check the bathroom. He knocked on the door, and waited for an answer, but none came. He opened the door to find that room also empty. Where could she be?

Winston began to worry that Sarain had left him in a fit of anger, like she had done in the past. He had no clue where she would go, and was unsure if her scent would still be strong enough to follow by now.

The sun was beginning to set, and Winston readied himself to go out and look for Sarain, when he heard the sound of his door creaking open. He rushed to the door to find Sarain on the other side, stepping in. She looked a bit surprised to find Winston so close to the door, and then quickly noticed the flustered expression on his face. "What's wrong?" she asked him. "Where have you been?" he quickly said.

Sarain stared at Winston for a moment, a look of hesitation in her eyes before she finally replied, "I thought you said I could come and go as I pleased?" Winston stared at her in disbelief, and then muttered, "That was before I realized how unsafe it is for you out there; there are people who would hurt or take advantage of you in your condition." "That's why I came back before it got dark," Sarain remarked.

Winston began to fill up with frustration, but he hesitated to argue with Sarain; she had technically done nothing wrong, but still he did not like the idea of her going out alone. He took a deep breath, and then calmly asked, "Where did you go?" She glanced at him for a second, as if trying to read his thoughts, before replying, "I just walked around." "Did you go to the marketplace?" he asked, his concern starting to show once again. Sarain stared at him, but did not answer his question, so Winston took this as a "yes", and then commented, "I don't want you going to the marketplace without me; it may be safer during the day, but not all bad things are limited to the night." She then looked him in the eyes as she said, "But you are, and sometimes I want to go out in the sun!" Her words were like a dagger into his heart; Winston was surprised to hear the new Sarain speak so harshly, and didn't know how to respond.

After about a minute of silence, Winston spoke by asking, "Did you talk to anyone?" Sarain glanced at him, again as if trying to read his thoughts, and then she answered with a simple, "No." Afterwards, she turned and walked away, going into her room, where she shut the door behind her. Winston continued to stand there, a little in shock, as he thought to himself, "She's lying."

A few hours went by with Winston sitting on the couch contemplating as Sarain avoided him by staying holed up in the bedroom, only leaving briefly to get food to bring back to the room. The whole thing felt like a childish spat, but Winston didn't know what to do or how to deal with the new Sarain. She didn't think knowledgably like the old one, but still had the same fiery spirit. Though even in his frustration, he could see why Sarain was so upset; she was tired of being cooped up, and the daylight was something a human being such as her needed to be in.

Winston began to feel as though sheltering this Sarain was his way of holding onto what he never had with the Sarain he knew and loved. He began to wonder if his taking care of her was really what was best for her, and he thought of how better off she would be in a community far away from Shaven; perhaps a small town full of humans and nothing else, and no one who would recognize her as the demon hunter he knew.

Winston tried to give it some thought, but wasn't sure how he would go about getting Sarain to such a place, or even if he was ready to let go of her just yet. The brown-eyed girl was his only tie to a dream he thought he had lost, and now that he had found her, he didn't want to stop dreaming.

She opened her eyes to find a bright shining white light that was almost blinding. She blinked a few times, letting her eyes adjust to the brightness, and when they finally did, she realized that she was standing in a park.

Sarain gazed around. The park was oddly familiar, but she couldn't place why. The ground was made of fine white sand that didn't seem to cling to her bare feet, and the sky was so blue that it didn't appear real. She took a few steps, expecting for her feet to sink into the sand, but they didn't. She then walked to the park's playground, where she found him waiting.

He sat, half swinging on the swing set, his hands gently gripping the silvery chain that held him up. He stared up at her with his hazel eyes, as though he knew she would come, and he motioned for her to sit on the swing next to him. Sarain complied, but did not swing; instead letting her feet hang and graze against the sand.

"You're going to have to be careful… and you can't lose your faith," he muttered. Sarain stared at the man, who no longer made eye contact, but she watched as his dark hair gleamed in the sunlight, and she knew that there was something familiar about this man too. He swayed back and forth, softly swinging with the gentle breeze, as Sarain admired his tanned skin. And as she peered at the man, she noticed something odd; for a split second, she could have sworn she saw a scar upon his neck, but the image was gone in a flash, leaving Sarain unsure if she had even seen it at all.

"He's a good man, you know... Even if he doesn't always seem to be," the man spoke again. Sarain listened intently, though her mind raced with questions. "You are so important now... Too important to give up...or to give in," he stated, and then he turned and looked at her as he asked, "You do understand?" She softly shook her head "no", but instead of getting upset, the man simply cracked a smile and said, "Don't worry, you will." The man began to get up to leave, when Sarain finally let herself ask him a question; "Who are you?"

The man turned back and stared down at her, with a loving expression upon his face as he answered, "A friend."

Sarain then for some reason unknown to her, closed her eyes, not wanting nor being able to bear to watch the man walk away. And he would indeed be gone before her eyes would open again.

Sarain felt overcome with a heavy emotion when she woke; her dream had left her feeling sad and confused. She thought of how she wanted to talk to someone about her dream, unsure if it was truly just a dream, or something much more important. Winston was the first person who came to mind, but then she recalled the awkwardness of the night before, and suddenly felt as though she couldn't talk to him about such a thing.

Sarain then thought of Father David, and how he had said that if she was ever looking for guidance, that she could come to him. She knew that he was virtually a stranger to her, but then again, with her amnesia, everyone was a stranger, leaving her unsure of whom she could trust, and surely a man of the church could be trusted above others. With that decided, Sarain only had to figure out how to sneak out of the house; certainly Winston wouldn't have let himself sleep in again so that Sarain could sneak out so easily once more.

Sarain crept out softly from her room, having opened the bedroom door as gently as she could. She tiptoed down the hallway and was surprised to see Winston, once again, sound asleep on the couch. She couldn't believe how easy this was going to be as she snuck towards the door. She then cracked it open and squeezed through; giving Winston one last glance, making sure he remained asleep. She saw that his eyes were still shut as she closed the door, and she turned and headed towards the town of Shaven, with a hope to find answers to the questions that she held.

Sarain walked the town quickly and cautiously, as though fearing that she might be followed. When she past the park, she stopped for only a moment, recalling her dream, but knowing that it wasn't this park that she had dreamt of.

As she arrived at the chapel, she pushed open its iron gate once more, and hurried up its stone steps. Once she reached its heavy double doors, she strained to get them open, but found that they were locked. Sarain took a step back, looking up at the large cross above her head, and wondering why the chapel doors would be locked. Was it too early?

Sarain contemplated waiting for someone to show up, but then she wasn't sure how long she wanted to be out, possibly making Winston worry if he were to wake and find her gone. She reluctantly started to head down the staircase when she suddenly heard someone call out, "Sarain?" She turned toward the voice to see Father David walking along the side of the chapel, a watering pail in hand.

"I didn't expect to see you back so soon" he spoke. "I was hoping I could discuss something with you, but then I found your doors locked," she replied. "Yeah we had someone vandalize the chapel last night," he stated. "Oh!" Sarain said with shock, "Is everything ok?" "More or less, the culprit just tossed stuff around, nothing too serious," David responded. "Do you get a lot of that kind of thing?" she asked curiously. "Not usually, I know that the town has kind of gone under the past year, but the criminal activity has been remarkably low lately. Last night's vandalism came as a shock to us," he stated.

"But enough about un-pleasantries, what did you come here to discuss?" David asked. Over the next few minutes, Sarain proceeded in telling him about her dream, going into extreme detail, as they sat on the steps leading up to the chapel. David listened intently, and when Sarain was done describing the dream, he stated, "It sounds as though you are starting to get your memory back." "But what does the dream mean?" she asked. "That is something only you can answer," he replied, "but it must be something of great importance, for the spirit of a loved one to come and visit you in a dream." "A spirit?" she said sounding surprised. "Well from what you described, it sounded like someone you once knew paid you a visit; dreams are the most common way that the dead speak to us," David explained.

Sarain was quiet for a moment, and then she finally said, "I wish I could remember him." "You will in time," David remarked, "But right now it's more important that you focus on what he told you; you need to keep your faith during this time, and trust that there is a greater plan for you, and that everything that has happened has happened for a reason." Sarain nodded her head in agreement, and turned to David with a smile on her face. She then placed her hand on top of his, and gave it a light squeeze as she said, "Thank you for listening to me; you don't know what it means to me to have someone to talk to." And as Sarain moved her hand away from his, she noticed that David had begun to blush, and she realized that as a priest, he might not be used to physical contact, especially from a woman. Sarain then too began to blush as she gave David an awkward half smile, and the two were silent for a while.

Neither of the two seemed to notice or even sense the heavily shrouded figure that watched them from the shadows in the distance, but his vibrant blue eyes glowed from within his hooded cloak.

The now irritated Winston turned and headed back down the darkened alley with the image of Sarain sitting on the steps of the church, holding the hand of another man scorched into his mind. All he could think of was "not again"; he could not lose her to another man, and as the idea began to infuriate him, Winston started to feel a fire growing inside him. Suddenly heat surged through his body, and Winston felt a searing pain pulsate in his skull. He gripped his head as he fell to his knees, letting out a deep groan of pain that bellowed from his gut. He clenched his teeth and balled his fists as he always did, as he waited for the feeling to pass, and once it did, he climbed back on his feet, and brushed himself off.

Winston hated every time that he was overcome by one of these strange seizures, but this was not the first; in fact, it was just one of many that he had had in the past year, and now they were beginning to become more frequent. Winston wasn't sure what was happening to him, but he knew that the problem started the night Aion force fed him his blood, the same night that Sarain had died, and he wasn't sure when it was going to end, or what he might become.

Chapter 7

Sarain parted ways with David, thanking him once again for listening to her, but this time being more careful not to touch him. Afterwards, Sarain headed back towards Winston's, trying to hurry, and hoping that he would still be sleeping.

The afternoon sun shined brightly up in the sky as Sarain hiked through the desert of Wormwood Alley. She still thought of her dream, wondering what it could mean, and if there truly was something important about her. She wondered when her memory would come back, what it would mean for her, and if it would change anything.

Winston's house came into view, and Sarain began to pick up her pace. She knew that their past interactions had been a bit coarse lately, but she found herself wanting to see Winston again, as though she were visiting with an old friend. When she reached his door, she took a deep breath, then slowly opened the door, and crept inside.

The first thing Sarain saw was that Winston was sitting upright on the couch, but he did not turn to look towards the door as she entered his house. Instead, Winston appeared to be staring out into space, and it wasn't until Sarain took a few steps closer, that she realized that he was actually staring at the dark stain on his floor. She glanced at the stain, remembering the flash of monsters she had seen when she touched it before, but then waved those thoughts away as she said to Winston in a soft tone, "I'm back, I hope you're not mad... I just needed to do something."

When Winston remained silent, Sarain took a few more steps toward him, and asked, "Is everything okay?" He was quiet and still for a moment longer, and then as if snapping out of a trance he got up, turned, and walked towards Sarain. As he approached her, he seemed to move almost robotic-like. Then suddenly he opened his arms, and wrapped them around Sarain in a stiff and awkward embrace. She didn't know how to respond, so she continued to let him hug her until finally he spoke, saying, "I'm just glad you're alright." "I'm sorry that I made you worry," Sarain muttered.

Winston continued to hold on to Sarain, pressing her body tightly against his, as he took a deep breath, inhaling in the scent of her hair. Sarain suddenly went stiff as she realized that Winston was smelling her, and then it hit her that he was trying to figure out where she had been. She then pushed him away, shooting him an angry look as she stomped off towards the bedroom, and then slammed the door behind her.

Winston sighed in relief, not because Sarain had left the room, but because she did not have the man's scent on her. Afterwards, he sat back down on the couch, glancing at his bloodstain on the floor, and began to think once again how much he had sacrificed for this one woman, this one frustrating woman.

The sun had long since set before Sarain stepped out of the bedroom again, only for her to find that Winston was gone for once. There was no note or clue to where he might have gone, and Sarain contemplated going out to look for him; but instead, she sat down on the couch and thought, "This is him trying to prove a point." It was obvious that Winston wanted to show her how it felt to be left in the dark. So Sarain sat and waited for him to return.

As she waited, she gazed down at the dark stain on the floor, wondering once again what could have caused such a nasty stain. She thought of the vision she saw the last time she had touched it, and wondered if it was some kind of fluke, or if it would happen again. Sarain found herself sliding off the couch, and kneeling on the ground, she extended her hand out to the stain and grazed her fingers along the ground once again. But this time nothing happened. Sarain pressed the palm of her hand against the stain, but still no vision. She sighed, figuring that the first time must have been some weird form of an overactive imagination, and she began to get up.

As she pulled herself off her knees and on to her feet, she began to feel herself growing dizzy. Perhaps she needed to eat something, or perhaps she got up too quickly, she thought, but soon the room was at a full spin. Sarain staggered for a moment, but it was the sound of voices shouting behind her that got her to spin around, and in her blurring haze, she saw a group of beasts had gathered in the living room. They appeared to be surrounding someone else, and paid no attention to Sarain. She realized that two of the beasts were holding a man down, and with her straining to focus on who it was, she heard the man say, "You might as well kill me, I'll never tell you where she is!"

Sarain gasped as she realized that she recognized the man's voice, it was Winston's. Impulsively, she shouted out, "Don't hurt him!" And still in a haze she saw the largest of the beasts, a gargoyle looking man with bat-like wings, turn and stare directly at her and then say, "Ahh, I see she is here," and followed by him yelling, "Grab her!"

Sarain then tensed up as she prepared herself to be seized by one of the creatures, and when she saw a beast lunge at her she nearly shrieked until she realized that there was no impact, but that instead the beast simply past through her. She then turned toward the sound of yet another struggle, only to see herself or at least someone who looked much like her, being yanked up by a couple of demons. Blood dripped from the other Sarain's mouth as she proceeded to argue with the bat-like man, but their words began to become indistinct to the hazy Sarain, who had started to hear a deafening high-pitch ring echoing throughout her ears.

She watched as the gargoyle approached the battered Winston with a sword raised, and gasped so hard that she nearly gagged when she saw him run Winston through with the blade. Winston's limp body fell into a pool of his own dark blood, and as Sarain quickly looked away, she saw her doppelganger screaming in anguish, and to her surprise, she saw the woman's eyes glowing an intense violet.

She's one of them, Sarain thought, and she came to the sudden revelation, "I'm one of them," she muttered as she collapsed with everything going black.

"Sarain! Wake up, Sarain!" a worried Winston cried out. Sarain groaned as she opened her eyes, and realized that she was lying on the floor in Winston's arms, and near the blood stained ground. "What happened?" Winston asked with concern, but Sarain did not reply. Seeming undisturbed by the fact that she had passed out, instead she franticly recalled her vision, and while gazing up at Winston, she said, "You almost died!"

He stared down at her with confusion as he stated, "What are you talking about, I'm fine." "No, not now," she replied and turned towards the stain on the floor and said, "Then." "Did you remember that?" Winston asked in amazement. Sarain nodded softly as she muttered, "Yes... I remembered you."

As Winston stared down at Sarain, she gazed up into his bright blue eyes, and saw a tear escape down his cheek. It was then that she came to a sudden realization, "Your friend.... I'm the one who died." Another tear fell from Winston's eyes as he mumbled, "It looks like you are," and then he lifted her up slightly as he embraced her in an emotional hug, his tears soaking against her skin.

As Winston's embrace continued, Sarain felt the skin of his cold cheek linger against her warm neck, and immediately she got a flash of him lying on top of her. It was a vision that only lasted a second in actuality, but for Sarain, it felt much longer; she saw Winston hovering above her, a loving yet vulnerable look was in his eyes. The cool skin of his chest was pressed again her warm bare breasts, and he caressed the nape of her neck with his fingertips before leaning down and softly kissing her skin.

Before the vision ended, Sarain saw how the two of them moved, heard how they moaned, and felt how they kissed. As she came out of the hallucination, Sarain saw the now present Winston staring down at her with confusion once again. "Did something just happen?" he asked. She continued to gaze up at him, as she felt herself blush, and while growing nervous, she asked, "Were we lovers?"

Winston let out a slight gasp as he hesitated to answer. Truth was, he wasn't sure what they had been at the point of Sarain's death, but as he looked down at the new Sarain, who had clearly just seen something from their past, he wondered what his answer could mean for their future. Every ounce of his being begged him to answer yes, but it was the word, "No" that finally escaped his lips.

Sarain sighed, and Winston wasn't sure if it was a sigh of relief or one of disappointment. He then helped Sarain climb up to her feet, whom still appeared to be a bit lightheaded. She swayed for a moment, and then stumbled as she tried to take a step. Winston immediately caught Sarain as she fell forward, colliding against him, and as he glanced down at her, once again in his arms, he saw her staring up at him curiously, as though seeing him in a new light. And he wondered if the innocent crush she had seemed to have on him a few days earlier had changed.

Was she going to go back to how she had been before she died, or had Sarain come back different? Winston wasn't sure what it was that he wanted, but he feared the outcome either way, because even if she was able to love him, what would that mean to them now that she was mortal?

Chapter 8

Winston helped Sarain get to bed early that night, with her being exhausted from the visions that she had had. Afterward, Winston decided to step outside into the cool night air, the sky filled with stars and the moon shining brightly.

His mind was racing with thoughts of Sarain, and while he couldn't understand how she had come back from the dead and why she was now human, he was glad to finally know that this indeed was Sarain and not just a look-a-like. A part of him was also excited to see that she was starting to remember her old life, even if it meant that the old unhappy memories came back too. Winston wanted Sarain to remember all that they had been through together, so that perhaps she would remember what they had meant to each other.

Winston looked out into the desolate desert surroundings; once upon a time, he had thought that this, Wormwood Alley, was a good place for him to live, but now that Sarain was back in his life, this bleak place seemed all wrong for her. He wanted her to live somewhere nice, somewhere peaceful, unlike anywhere she had lived. Winston knew that Sarain had spent many of her years in slums and broken down neighborhoods, where she could afford live or squat while she cleared that city of its demonic life. And what he knew of her childhood and her days traveling with her grandfather and their clan, they had been nomadic and lived in camps.

Winston wanted the cliché white picket fence, green grass, and big house for Sarain, but he knew that he couldn't give it to her. As long as she was with him, he knew her life would be filled with demonic things, long nights, and a basic avoidance of human society. Winston wanted Sarain to have a shot at a real life, and now that she was human, she had a true chance at just that. But at the same time, he felt that he still wasn't ready to let go of her just yet, because his dream life was to have her in his.

Winston gazed out into the night, wondering if Sarain could ever find peace in his quiet dark world. Suddenly, as if the world was giving him an answer, Winston spotted a single white flower blooming from a lone spot of the ground. It grew out from rocks where nothing else would grow. Winston approached the flower, unsure of what kind it was, it looked to be more than just a common weed or wildflower, and it flourished so that he believed that it must have been a night-blooming only flora.

As Winston bent down to smell the flower's sweet scent, for a moment, he heard the crunch of pebbles grinding into the ground. He quickly looked up and scanned his surroundings, but saw no one. His curiosity began to peak and Winston wondered if he was not alone, and as he began to step away from the flower and toward the direction of the sound, he immediately saw a bird fly out from behind a bush and quickly flutter away. Winston sighed when he realized that all was silent again, and that perhaps his life wasn't as dangerous for Sarain as he had first thought. Then he turned back to the flower and swiftly plucked it from the ground.

Winston proceeded to head back to his house, his senses clouded by thoughts of the lovely Sarain sleeping serenely inside, that the sound of pebbles shifting once again went unnoticed.

Sarain woke early the following morning; feeling well rested, she stretched her arms and legs out from under the bed's covers, and then she rolled onto her side and quickly noticed that lying next to her on the pillow was single white flower. Winston, she thought, and then recalled the events of the night before, and began to feel herself nearly blush as she thought of Winston again.

Sarain brought the flower to her nose and inhaled its sweet scent, and then she found herself wondering how many other times she may have done such a thing in the past. She wondered when or if she would have another vision, hoping that her memory in its entirety would return soon. And then she realized that if her memory did come back, that that would mean that she would remember her death too.

Her death; how was such a thing feasible? Sarain began to think about her existence, and how it was even possible; she remembered her dream, and the man telling her how she was special, and now she began to understand what he meant. Someone coming back from the dead had to be entirely extraordinary, but Sarain couldn't figure what it was about her that was so unique and deserving of such a miracle. Then she thought of David, and how his religious insight might have an answer for her, and she wondered if Winston would be okay with her going out again.

Sarain quickly dressed, and picked up the flower from her bed. She carefully carried it out and into the living room where Winston slept. For a moment, she contemplated waking him up to let him know her plans to go out, but as she watched him sleeping peacefully, she decided against waking the man, and instead gently placed the flower on his chest, hoping that he would see it as a gesture of kindness. Afterwards, she quietly crept out the door and into the daylight. Sarain started her almost routine walk to the town of Shaven, her destination being the church.

She moved fast in her pace today, not wanting to leave Winston alone for long, and desperately wanting David's opinion on her latest foresights into her background. Sarain didn't bother to stop and watch anyone or anything, she didn't care to make eye contact, or observe her surroundings; she just hurried with only her goal in mind. When she reached the Church of the Warrior, she raced up the steps, and glided past the angel statue. She reached for the double doors and found them unlocked once again. With a sigh of relief she opened up the doors, with them creaking out a heavy groan, and then rushed into the chapel, immediately calling out, "Father David!"

David was kneeling in a pew, praying, when Sarain busted in, and quickly turned around at the sound of his name, looking astonished. "Sarain… Another visit? This is beginning to become a daily occurrence with you," he stated. "I hope you don't mind, but I have more questions," she replied. "I kind of figured as much," David responded. "I know I've been an inconvenience lately, but something significant has happened to me," Sarain pleaded. David then smiled, shaking his head slightly, and said, "You've not been an inconvenience, I'm glad to be of help, now tell me, what troubles you?"

"I've started remembering my past, and I've been seeing it in visions," she relayed. "Well that is a bit strange, but not uncommon in your condition, especially if there is something to trigger your memory," David remarked. "Maybe so, but I also remember something else, or at least realized it… I… I think I died," Sarain stammered out.

This time David wasn't so quick to reply, instead he sat down and thought for a moment, with Sarain waiting for him to tell her that she must have been mistaken, and then to her surprise, David turned to her and said, "Then perhaps you truly are here to do great things." "So you believe me?" she asked with astonishment. "I understand that this town has a heavy supernatural element here, one to which I could never fully understand. So in answer to your question, yes, I do believe you," David replied. "Have you ever heard of this happening before? Is there anything that you could tell me that might help me figure out what I'm supposed to be doing?" Sarain questioned with anxiety. "The only other time I've heard of such an event happening is with our lord and savior, Jesus Christ… Now I'm not saying that you're his second coming, but if you have truly come back from the dead, than there is a very good reason for it, and you must keep your eyes and ears open for a sign from God on what it is that he wants you to do," David preached. "How will I know it when I see it?" she asked curiously. "That is only for you to determine; I cannot help you there," he replied.

Sarain sighed and then took a seat on one of the pews. Her thoughts were racing, and as if sensing her frustration, David stated, "You died, but you were never dead." She looked up at him with confusion as she asked, "What do you mean?" "The body is just our mortal shell, and when we die, our immortal soul goes on. I imagine yours didn't go that far, just far enough to see that you were still needed here, and I'm sure in a life such as yours, something like that isn't so hard to grasp," David remarked. "But how did I come back?" Sarain asked. "Why question the method, when it's the result that you need to focus on?" he answered.

Sarain sighed yet again, and knew that David was right; she needed to find out why she was back.

Chapter 9

Sarain hurried home after her visit with David, hoping that Winston wouldn't be too upset with her. The sun still shined brightly up in the sky, and it was possible that he could still be sleeping; but given the events following the last few times Sarain had gone out, she expected to find Winston awake, and likely in a foul mood.

She raced through the desert landscape only to stop and pause outside Winston's door, wondering what she would find inside, until finally Sarain's hand went to the latch, and she slowly pushed the door open. She stepped inside and immediately saw that Winston was sitting up on the couch. As Sarain stepped closer, she noticed that a sword was lying across his lap, and she immediately asked, "What is that for?" Winston turned to look at her as he stated, "If you insist on going out alone, then I think it's time that you learn how to fight again." "Oh," she responded, a bit surprised, and then she asked, "Now?" Winston then nodded with a smirk, "Yes, now. I'll show you the basics here inside, and then once it's dark, we can train outside."

Winston stood up and walked around the couch, towards Sarain. He extended the sword in his hand to her and said, "Take it." Sarain reached out, hesitantly, and took hold of the sword's hilt. Winston then let go of the blade, letting Sarain take the weight of the whole sword. Its weight surprised her at first, she hadn't expected such a slender blade to be so heavy, and she quickly placed her other hand on the hilt as well. And as she held the sword, she felt a sensation spread over her entirety; it was a strange sort of calmness, as though the weapon was an appendage that Sarain had been missing.

Winston stepped behind Sarain, and then placed his arms around her, and on top of her own arms and hands. He then lowered his head until his cheek was against hers, "Separate your hands," he whispered into her ear, "Don't lay them over each other, place them apart, to sturdy your grip," he added, and then showed her by moving her hands with his. Sarain could feel the coolness of Winston's chest against her back, even through their clothes, and his hands were cold against hers; but instead of his skin giving her chills, Sarain began to feel herself becoming aroused. She suddenly recalled her vision from the previous night, and despite what Winston had said about them not being lovers, she knew that they must have made love at least once.

Sarain did her best to ignore the urges that were stirring inside her, and focused on the training that Winston was giving her. They went over different stances for many situations; Winston showed her what was best for charging an opponent and what was best for being charged upon. Each time he used his hands to guide her body into the position it needed to be in to fulfill the scenario that he had given. After a while, Winston told Sarain to take a break, even though she was excited to learn more. Training with Winston not only felt familiar to Sarain, but it also felt fulfilling.

During this break, Sarain ate lightly as Winston examined the weapons he kept, as though debating what he wanted to teach her next. She finished a piece of bread as she saw Winston peer out the door, and then state, "Okay I think it's time to take your training outside." She nodded and then quickly followed Winston outside, carrying the sword he had given her earlier. Once they were both outside, Sarain noticed that Winston clutched a sword of his own, in his hand, and she quickly asked, "Are you going to spar against me?" Winston smiled at the seemingly obvious answer to her question, as he said, "Well that is the plan, but don't worry, I'll start off slow."

Winston walked past her and took a fighting stance some yards away. He turned to Sarain and stated, "I want you to charge me, but make sure to keep your blade down and out. Don't run at me with your sword raised; that's a classic fighting mistake because it leaves you open to an attack." "Okay," Sarain said with a nod, and on Winston's cue, she rushed toward him with her sword in hand. She charged toward him and almost simultaneously, he blocked her strike as she attacked. Sarain took a step back, and Winston immediately said, "I want you to charge me again." She nodded once more, and raised her sword, but instead of running at him, Sarain jumped towards Winston with her sword thrust outward. He quickly dodged this attack, and simply replied, "Good," then came at Sarain with his own assault.

It was in this moment that Sarain had a sudden flash to her and Winston fighting back to back, surrounded by beasts. The image only lasted a second, and afterward, she found herself quickly blocking his attack. Winston continued to rush her, but as he did so, Sarain began to see his face blur, and for a moment he resembled the man who spoke to her in her dream days ago, only younger. Sarain shook the image away, trying to focus on her training, and blocking yet another of Winston's attacks.

Sarain swung her sword with it clanging against Winston's; she did this instinctively, but she began to notice that he was putting more effort into his attacks, and she wondered if this was to keep up with her training or just to keep up with her. Sarain soon found herself running backwards, as she blocked multiple attempts that Winston made to swing his blade at her, and it felt as though he was putting in a lot of energy into his attacks.

Sarain begin to feel her heart race, and she suddenly swung her sword at Winston with her full strength. His blade quickly shot up and clanged against her steel, but she didn't let up, instead she pressed her weight against her blade, trying to force Winston back. And once Winston began to feel the strain of Sarain fighting him for real he immediately stated with shock and confusion, "What are you trying to do?"

Winston then used much of his strength to shove back against her blade, and Sarain suddenly fell back, tumbling to the ground. In a moment of horror for Winston, he watched as Sarain sprawled out as she fell, dropping her sword away from herself, and then striking her head on a medium sized rock that lay on the ground. She lay motionless for a second before the shock wore off Winston, and he rushed to her side. He lifted her head up in his arms, as he shouted, "Sarain! Are you okay? Can you hear me?" It was then that he felt the drops of warm sticky blood on the palm of his hand, and he realized that Sarain was bleeding from the back of her head. He stared down at her with fear; her eyes were closed and she continued not moving. "Wake up, Sarain!" he hollered down at her, and then he began to see her eyelashes flutter.

Everything was blurry as Sarain slowly opened her eyes, with Winston's voice sounding distorted and far away. She began to close her eyes once more, with everything feeling so strange and her feeling tired, but as she did so, she heard a voice cry out, "Wake up, my child!" This didn't sound like the voice of Winston, but instead of a woman. Sarain's eyes immediately shot open, and for a moment she saw a woman standing behind Winston, looking down at her. She had dark hair and dark eyes and bore a resemblance to Sarain herself, and as Sarain reached up towards the woman, she saw a soft smile spread across her face. Sarain tried to return the smile, but suddenly felt her body begin to thrash as she felt herself go into overload.

Winston held onto Sarain tightly as she appeared to seize, hoping to keep her from further hurting herself during her convulsion. Sarain stared up into space as a wave of thoughts and knowledge flooded her, and she witnessed several images and scenes unfold before her very eyes. Memories began rushing back to her like tidal waves: she saw flashes of her clan's massacre, her childhood with Orran, her saving Kit, lounging with Eddie, fighting demons, and kissing Winston goodbye. The memories didn't stop there: she saw her grandfather Delmar, her father Aion, and her mother Ariana, until finally she saw everything. All her memories came back at once, and Sarain was overwhelmed, and then as she blinked her eyes a few times, she suddenly felt as though she had just woken from a dream.

Sarain lifted herself up from Winston's arms, with him quickly muttering, "Don't move so quick, you need to take it slow." She gazed around at her surroundings for a moment, and then turned and looked at Winston, and muttered his name, "Winston," almost as if confused. "Are you okay?" he asked her curiously. Sarain stared at him in disbelief, unsure how to answer, before finally responding, "I'm fine." She then helped herself up, against Winston's liking, and headed for the house. Winston quickly picked up their blades and hurried after her, but as he stepped inside his house, he heard the sound of the bedroom door slamming. He stood there in confusion, unsure if Sarain was mad at him or just tired.

Winston put the swords away, and after taking a moment to contemplate, he finally decided to check on Sarain by knocking on her door. There was no answer so next Winston decided to call out, "Sarain? Are you alright?" His hand slowly began to turn the doorknob, but stopped when he heard her reply, "I'm tired... I'm going to bed." He then let go of the knob, still concerned for Sarain, but not wanting to disturb her.

Sarain listened as Winston walked away from her door, she held onto herself, and cradled her legs, her knees pressed against her chest. She took a deep breath, as she tried to stop herself from shaking.

She remembered everything, and now she wished that she could forget it again.

Chapter 10

Sarain spent most of the night quietly crying, hoping that Winston wouldn't hear; and when he didn't come to her door at all that night, she knew that he hadn't heard her. She cried over her regained memories. She cried for her mother, Kit, Eddie, and Orran; and she realized now that her departed friends had been visiting her in her dreams the past few days.

Sarain felt lost, and she no longer knew what to do with herself; she had spent so many years seeking revenge, and now with Aion gone, a life of just hunting simple demons seemed both pointless and unfulfilling. Sarain couldn't fathom why she had come back from the dead, and a part of her wished she hadn't, but there was another part of her that was glad to have a second chance, even if she didn't know what to do with it.

Sarain then thought of Winston and his utter loyalty to her; and though she wasn't surprised, a part of her was still amazed to see how much Winston was devoted to her and her memory after all this time. She thought of how she had treated Winston in the past, regretting having abandoned him so many years ago, and she thought of how differently he was living now from just a year ago; his home had turned to shambles, and he no longer kept company with women, and Sarain realized that this was because of her. Winston had evidently spiraled into a depression after she had died, and was now putting all his energy into helping her cope, now that she was back.

As Sarain thought about Winston, a faint smile began to spread across her lips; it was obvious that he still loved her, even when he tried to hide it from Sarain when he had thought that she might just be a look-a-like. His concern for her was much more than that of a worried friend. Sarain thought of Winston as her rock and with him by her side, she knew that she could adapt to her new life as a mortal. And though she had only known about her demon blood for the past few years of her life, she felt a great difference in her being now; she now felt a vivid force inside of her, bursting with energy, instead of the draining hatred she had once been fueled by, which was likely amplified by the demonic blood.

Sarain finally fell asleep with thoughts of the many possibilities her life now held; no longer hiding or chasing someone, Sarain was now free from any obligation she once held. Sarain had peacefully irrelevant dreams that morning, and when she woke a few hours later, around noon, she began to recall the events of the day before and remembered why she had rushed to the exclusion of her room; the overwhelming memories and sudden realities of her new life were much to bear. Everything felt unreal, and though Sarain knew she was safe now, and no longer had to worry about a fierce life-threatening and oncoming battle, a part of her wasn't able to settle, as if still waiting for the other shoe to drop.

Sarain rose from her bed and quickly dressed. She knew that Winston was likely waiting outside her bedroom with questions, but she wasn't ready to give him the answers he sought. Instead, Sarain craved fresh air, and as she opened her door, she crept down the hallway hoping not to wake a sleeping Winston on the couch. But as she stepped into the living room, she soon saw that the couch was empty.

"You don't have to sneak out; you're free to come and go as you please, remember?" Winston muttered from his seat at the kitchen table. "Oh… Okay," Sarain weakly replied, and then walked towards the door, but stopped when Winston quickly stated, "I'd prefer if you'd carry a weapon with you though." "I'd rather not lug one around…I don't exactly have your abnormal strength you know," she remarked. Winston sighed, and then commented, "Well if that's the case, then go into the second drawer of my desk," he said pointing towards the corner of the room where it sat. Sarain thought that his request was a bit odd, but complied anyway, and when she pulled out the drawer she found herself catching her breath. She stared down into the drawer and saw a familiar object; it was her ankh, and she realized that Winston must have gone back to that mountaintop searching for her to have found it. She felt her eyes wanting to well up, but fought the urge to cry, because if she did, she knew that Winston would realize that she had gotten her memory back, and she wasn't ready to face him on that subject. Instead, Sarain swallowed down her emotions and falsely asked, "What is it?" "It's something that used to belong to you; a relic that wards off unnatural creatures that might do you harm," Winston answered.

Sarain stared down at her ankh for a while, hesitating to touch it, remembering the last time she wore it, when it burned her. She had worn that ankh for years, ever since her mother had given it to her as a child. It felt as though it was something in her past, something she had outgrown, but she knew that Winston was right to suggest her wearing it. Still, she hesitated to touch the ankh, but she knew that if she waited much longer, then Winston would grow suspicious, so she finally decided to pick the pendant up. She lifted it up first by the chain that Winston must have had someone repair, because she was pretty sure she had broken it when she had ripped it off her neck a year ago. She wondered how he managed to carry the pendant down the mountain top with the fact that it should have not only burned him but likely turned his stomach to even be near it; and she knew that it must have been because of his dedication to her.

Sarain unhooked the clasp, and then lifted the chain up and behind her neck, and suddenly and in a familiar fashion, she fastened the pendant around her neck. The ankh fell upon her chest, as it had so many times before, and while a part of Sarain expected to be burned like she had the last time she wore it, the rest of her quickly felt at ease with the weight of the ankh upon her skin like it always had been. She then turned to Winston and asked, "Am I good to go out?" "If that is what you wish," he replied, without asking any more questions. "Okay... I won't be long, I promise, I just want some fresh air... And since its safer for me out in the daylight..." she stated without finishing her sentence; Winston had already turned away from her, and Sarain wasn't sure if he wasn't interested in her statement or just purposely trying to ignore her. Either way, Sarain cracked open the door and squeezed out, not hearing the sigh of discontent Winston gave after she left.

Sarain took a deep breath of air as she closed the door behind her; half from relief of no longer having to pretend in front of Winston, and half glad to be out in the open, amongst nature. She felt now, more than ever, that she had taken for granted the purity and fulfillment that she felt being out in the open; she had become so used to hunting when she was outside, that the world's everyday beauties had escaped her within the last few years of her life. Now she finally had the time to appreciate them.

Sarain walked aimlessly out in the wilderness, not sure where to go, but glad that she could venture out at all. She knew it was best to steer clear of the marketplace, and now with her memory back, she knew how to get into town without going through the supernatural swap meet. She crept through Shaven, sticking to the shadows, like she had always done throughout her life. She wasn't sure where she wanted to go; she just knew that she didn't want to go home.

Eventually Sarain found her way to the park, which was busted up and abandoned. Everywhere she looked appeared to be covered in graffiti; the only bench that wasn't was smashed up and appeared to have been torn up out of its cemented base in the ground. Sarain walked past it, and opted to sit on the curb instead, pondering over how much the small town had changed in just a year. Was this all just because of the demonic life that Sarain had rid from the town? Had it chased away the possible good supernatural life from the town as well? Sarain never thought that Aion could have ever brought anything good to anywhere, but perhaps she had overlooked something.

She sighed, knowing that it didn't matter now; one thing she knew best in life was that nothing could ever truly be undone; there would always be scars or some remnants of what had happened. Just as Sarain knew that though she may have been given a second chance of life, she wasn't the same as she was before. Not only was she mortal now, but it felt as though another part of her, a part of her essence, was gone too.

Sarain didn't know how to live a normal life, and felt as though she was now too old to learn. She thought of Winston, and how his strength was keeping her going, and while that seemed great now, she knew that with him and his vil sang lifestyle, she could never truly lead a normal life, and how the two being together would only get harder in the future. Sarain pondered over her friendship with Winston, wondering how it may one day hurt the both of them, and while she regretted ever leaving his side years ago, a part of her felt as though it would be best if she left again.

Sarain sighed at the complexity that was her life. She began to get up when she heard a voice say, "How odd to run into you here." She quickly turned her head around to see David standing nearby. "Father David!" she said with surprise, and he gave a chuckle, and asked, "Is it that strange to see me outside of the chapel grounds?" "It is, a little," Sarain admitted, with a half-smile, and then asked, "What brings you here today?" "Well you're not the only one who likes to go on walks, apparently," he replied, "Sometimes it feels good to go where others won't recognize me, but I guess I've been recognized after all." "Sorry about that, Father," she responded with David quickly saying, "Please, call me David; there is no need for formalities, especially outside of the chapel." "Of course…David," Sarain said with a smirk, and then remarked, "That actually feels more natural, anyway, since I'm pretty sure that you're younger than me and calling you father just seems strange." David then looked at Sarain with puzzlement as he stated, "I know I'm young to be a priest, but you don't look like you could be older than me; I'm twenty-four." "I'm in my thirties," Sarain replied. David looked stunned for a moment, and then said, after taking some time to think, "I guess I shouldn't be surprised by your youthfulness, since you already have come back from the grave; age defying looks really isn't that big of a deal after that." Sarain laughed and replied, "I've never really looked at it like that, but I guess you're right."

David then sat down on the curb next to where Sarain stood, causing her to sit back down where she had been before, now next to him. David sighed looking up at the mostly clear blue sky, and said, "It really is a beautiful day," then turned to Sarain and asked, "You've gotten your memory back, haven't you?" Sarain stared at him in amazement, and replied, "Yes, how did you know?" "You commented on your age, when you knew little about yourself before…Besides, you have a different quality about you; almost majestic," David responded. "How so?" she asked curiously. "It's your aura; I've only sensed such an aura before from those who have dedicated decades of their life to a purer existence of isolation and worship. Who exactly are you?" he spoke with awe. "I was a hunter, but now I don't know who I am," Sarain answered halfheartedly. "What's stopping you from doing the work you did before?" he asked. "I lack the strength…and the will. I'm not the same person I was in that life," she explained.

David looked Sarain in the eyes as he asked, "And what kind of person are you now?" She sighed after a moment of silent contemplation, and said, "I don't know."

"Hmm," was his mere response, and then David asked, "Well who were you before you were a hunter?" "I was a child, a member of a nomadic clan, until I became an orphan," she answered. "Nomadic and an orphan? That doesn't leave you with many roots. What was your family like?" he both remarked and questioned. "My mother was the clan healer, until she was murdered by her father, who was also the one who raised me," she stated. "And your father," he pried. "I didn't know him until the last few years of my life…and he was an abomination of God," she told David, who looked puzzled, so Sarain then remarked, "Let's just leave it at that."

"Well, with that aside, even just growing up an orphan can make one struggle with their identity; I should know, since I'm an orphan myself," David proclaimed, and then relayed, "My mother was a prostitute, and left me on the steps of a monastery one day when she decided that she was tired of feeding me, and I never knew my father. But the monks there raised me and trained me in their ways, until the day that I took my own holy vows. I don't focus on where I came from; such a thing is out of our control anyway. What's important is who you choose to be; if you feel that you are no longer a hunter, then what is it you wish to be?"

Sarain thought for a while, pondering what it was that she wanted out of life, but all she could bring herself to say was, "I don't know."

Chapter 11

Sarain and David chatted a little while longer, recanting what they could remember of their lives before they had lost their families. David's life with his mother had been cruel and bleak, while what Sarain remembered of her mother was peaceful. But both of their lives dramatically changed after the loss of their mothers; Sarain's became full of strife, while David found purpose in the monastery.

They parted ways after their conversation, with David needing to get back to the chapel. Sarain, who now felt a little more clear-minded, knew she should head home, both before it got dark, and so Winston wouldn't worry about her being gone so long.

She kept a steady pace, not stopping for anything. The once blue sky had turned orange and purple as the sun began to set. Sarain quickened her steps, hoping to beat the sun home before it could turn night. She felt her ankh bounce against her chest as she started to jog home; she knew that it would help ward off any possible demons she may come upon, but it wouldn't necessarily stop them. Sarain wasn't sure if she could match a beast in battle any longer, especially unarmed, but she knew that nighttime didn't automatically mean a demon would find her, and Shaven seemed to have a lot less of them than it had before. Still, Sarain hurried to get home.

It was almost completely dark out once she reached Winston's door; the sun could barely be seen behind the mountains; it was a time that some of the bolder demons might start their hunt. As Sarain opened the door, she prepared herself for a likely angry Winston. The door groaned as she swung it ajar, and stepped inside. The first thing she heard as she entered the house was Winston frantically shouting, "Do you realize how late it is? I was going to go out looking for you, just like any other demon-blooded creature could have!"

Sarain sighed, expecting to have yet another argument with Winston, when suddenly something on the table caught her eye. In a small clear vase, half full of water, was the flower Winston had given her the day before. Sarain wasn't sure when Winston had placed it there on the table, but even with the care he had given it, the flower had already started to wilt. The blossom still looked full and beautiful, but it had begun to droop.

Sarain gazed at the flora for a moment, ignoring Winston's annoyed stare, while thinking of how delicate life was. She then turned to him and stated, "There's something I have to tell you." Winston, seeing the seriousness in her face, immediately went quiet and grew concerned. "I remember…everything," she stammered out softly. Winston's eyes went wide, and he asked with confusion, "This happened while you were out?" "No," Sarain answered, hesitantly, "This happened after I blacked out last night." Suddenly Winston's brow grew heavy and tense as he said with a shaky voice, "So last night and today; you've been pretending with me, and avoiding me?" "I needed time to think," she quickly replied. "About what?" he shouted, "About how now that you're all back to normal you don't need me anymore!" "I didn't say that!" Sarain shouted back. Winston then shook his head, and stated, furiously, "I can't believe this!"

He stormed past Sarain, and out the door. She quickly followed after him, yelling, "Where are you going?" "Anywhere, but here!" he irately responded, and quickened his pace. Sarain tried to catch up to him, but was no match for his demon speed, and soon found herself standing outside alone. She groaned angrily, and kicked at the ground. She then headed back into the house, knowing that she was no longer skillful enough to track Winston down.

With nothing else she could do, Sarain sat down on the couch, and waited for Winston to return, all the while thinking that Winston must have felt the same kind of helplessness earlier that day as she did now, and maybe in that very same spot.

Hours went by while Sarain remained waiting on the couch for Winston to return. Out of boredom, she reached around her neck and unhooked the chain for her ankh. She held it out with one hand while the ankh dangled in front of her eyes. She stared at the old pendant, wondering how its power worked. Was it blessed? Or was it just the symbol alone that held its power? Sarain never really did understand how the ankh worked, just that it did. She knew that the symbol was heavily used in ancient Egyptian culture, but she wasn't sure why it harmed demons. She remembered when the ankh once burnt her; as she had finally turned into a vil sang the pendant had seared her skin. Nothing about it had felt holy, or even miraculous, it had just simply turned hot as though heated by a flame.

"So I guess you knew what that was all along," Winston remarked, his voice catching Sarain so off guard that she flinched and dropped the ankh. She hadn't heard the door open, and she quickly turned around to see Winston standing only a few feet away from her. "You're back," Sarain spoke with surprise, "Does that mean that you're no longer mad at me?" "No, I'm still mad that you basically lied to me…But I understand why you felt the need to think things through; you've been through a lot," Winston replied.

Sarain sighed, letting her gaze fall to the ground and settle upon her ankh, but she made no motion to pick it up. There was an awkward silence for a while, before Winston finally spoke again. "Do you remember where you went after you died?" he asked curiously. She shook her head first before answering, "No… I remember nothing…. There was nothing." She was quiet for a moment longer before she added, "I remember burning up, and then the next thing I knew, it was raining and I was digging my way out of the ground." "Hmm," Winston hummed as if struck with a revelation, which caused Sarain to ask, "What?" "You'd think that if there was a heaven, you would have gone there with everything you've done," he stated. "I'm not sure if it works that way…with me coming back and all," Sarain remarked.

"And no idea how you pulled that one off either?" he asked inquisitively. She shook her head again, "Not a clue."

Winston sighed with disappointment, and then he walked around the back of the sofa, purposely avoiding the ankh on the ground, and sat down on the other side of Sarain. He turned to her and asked, "What now? Are you going to go back to hunting?" Sarain pondered over the question, and answered, "I don't think I can; my strength is gone; I'm weaker now than I've been in a long time. And even still, I don't think I want to hunt anymore. With Aion finally dead, my motivation is gone." "There are other demons out there," Winston said matter-of-factly. "And there are other hunters who can take care of them," she replied. "So that's it?" he asked surprised. "That's it," she muttered in response.

Winston's gaze then fell to the ground, and Sarain noticed a look of sadness on his face causing her to ask, "What's wrong?" "You don't need me anymore," he simply said, and then went further on to explain, "Without all the hunting and battles, you can lead a normal life; you don't need my help for that." "I guess that means you can go about your life again too," Sarain commented, "Fix this place up back to the way it was, and find yourself another blood companion." Winston let out a small chuckle in response to her statement. "What's so funny?" Sarain intriguingly asked. "The fact that you think it's that easy," Winston replied with a smirk on his face. "Hey, as I recall, you never had any problem getting women," she remarked, "In fact, I'm surprised you're not with someone now." "But I am with someone," he stated, causing Sarain to suddenly stare at him in disbelief, until he added, "I'm here with you."

Sarain rolled her eyes, muttering, "You know what I mean." "I know," Winston said with a smile, and then his face went serious as he said, "But you're my girl… There are no other women for me." Sarain's breath caught in her throat, and she turned and gazed at Winston, stunned, but didn't say a word. He stared at her intently as he spoke, "I know a lot has happened with us, and I know Orran's death must still feel fresh for you, but if you think that you could ever feel that way for me…" He then trailed off, as though hearing the words out loud suddenly sounded as though he were asking too much of her. Winston then shook his head, and said, "Never mind, I'm asking too much of you; you need a normal life." He got up from the couch and began walking back towards the door, when Sarain said, "Are you kidding me?" Winston then stopped in his tracks, and turned back toward her. "I was in love with you before Orran died," Sarain stated ironically.

Winston's mouth dropped, and it took him a moment to muster up the coherency, to say, "Are you serious?" "Why do you think I sent you away when I went after Aion; I couldn't stand the thought of losing you again," she told him. His eyes began to tear up while Sarain continued to say, "Orran may have been my first crush and oldest friend, but I've never loved anyone the way I love you."

Tears rolled down Winston's cheeks, as he stood there shaking. He gazed at her in disbelief, and then muttered, "Say it again." Sarain then gave Winston a sweet smile as she said, "I love you." Immediately, he rushed over to Sarain, his heart feeling so full that he almost thought it was going to start beating again. He quickly took Sarain into his arms, slightly catching her off guard with his speed. Without hesitation, he kissed her passionately, his salty tears upon their lips. Winston's arms held her tightly, as Sarain kissed him back, and when their lips finally parted, she stared up at him with intensity, and said, "Make love to me."

It was a request that he would not deny her. Winston lifted Sarain up into his arms, and carried her to the bedroom, where he gently laid her down on the bed. As Winston proceeded to climb onto the bed, he was quickly met with Sarain hungrily kissing him. She slipped her hands behind his neck, and pulled him in for the kiss, and when it broke, she abruptly pulled his shirt off over his head. Winston let out a chuckle in response to how anxious Sarain seemed to be. "What's so funny?" she asked smiling. "You. I never thought that I could make you this excited," he replied. Sarain ran her hands down Winston's chest, to his abs, and then stopped at the top of his pants where she gripped. "Do you have any idea how much I've thought about this?" she remarked. He smiled at her, and answered, "Yeah, actually I do."

It had been more than ten years since the one and only time they had ever made love, and it was a night that Winston had been forever replaying in his head since. A part of him worried that his years of dreaming and fantasizing over the last time they were together wouldn't live up to the real thing; and partly he was right, because the real thing turned out to be so much more than it was before. Their passion and desire for each other had grown stronger than it was previously, so many years of longing for one another.

They moaned, and Sarain continuously pulled Winston to her for more, her stamina surprising him. Their naked bodies moved and entwined as one, while he kissed and caressed every part of her, making her quiver. Every time Sarain held on to him, Winston felt as though she didn't want to let go of him, and he was right. It was a long while before they would finish, but when they did, they held each other, damp with sweat. Sarain laid there, exhausted, half on Winston, and half next to him. One of her legs was wrapped around his and her breasts pressed against his side as she clung to him with her arms. Winston's arm lay under and around Sarain's waist, as the other cradled her arm.

Winston lay there, drowsy, listening to Sarain's breathing slowing down, until she fell asleep, and then he whispered to her, "You are my everything," before finally falling asleep himself. That night they slept in each other's arms, and slept more soundly than either had ever before.

Sarain woke early the next morning with a sleeping Winston at her side. She felt her stomach growl, and knew that she was hungry and famished from the long night of love making. She slowly climbed out of bed not wanting to disturb Winston's peaceful slumber. Sarain crept out of the room and down the hall, and she headed for the kitchen where she grabbed the first thing of food that she could find, a half loaf of bread. She took it to the table, where she sat down and began to eat. As she ate, she found herself staring out in front of her where her eyes settled on the flower that she had seen the day before. The blossom had wilted considerably more since the last time she had gazed upon it; a couple of petals had fallen, while the rest began to brown, and the bud drooped heavily.

Sarain sighed in disappointment, the flower had been beautiful, and was such a lovely gesture from Winston that she was sad to see that it had died so quickly. Sarain reached out and lifted the flower out of the vase, preparing to throw the dead plant away. She stared at it for a moment longer, in her hand, with a sweet smile upon her face. As she held the stem, she closed her eyes, and thought of her love for Winston, happy that she had at last mustered the courage to tell him how she felt. She loved him so much that it felt as though her love radiated throughout her body, and when she opened her eyes again, she was shocked to what she found before her. The flower no longer was wilted, but instead flourished with its petals restored to the crisp white that they had been days before.

Sarain had healed it, like her mother had healed so many things long before.

Part 2

Chapter 12

Many weeks had passed since Sarain made her declaration of love to Winston, and every day since had been spent with them blissfully happy; making love throughout the night and sleeping in each other's arms throughout the day. They talked of old times, they joked, and they played, running around like free spirits. Winston continued to train Sarain in combat, regardless of the fact that she no longer wanted to hunt, but wanting her to stay safe in case a situation were to ever pop up when he wasn't by her side to protect her, though often their sparring turned into love play which usually ended in the bedroom.

Sarain and Winston constantly kissed; she would grab him and pull him in for a kiss every chance she got, sometimes surprising him around corners or during quiet moments. They only ever parted when Sarain would take her occasional daytime walks, or when Winston would hunt wildlife to feed on. Otherwise, they shopped together to get Sarain's food, and even occasionally went to the marketplace where Winston would keep a watchful eye on everyone around them. They bathed together, soaping one another up, slept together, and took long moonlit walks together. Life was indeed bliss for the two of them.

One day as Sarain dressed to go out for one of her day time walks, Winston sat at the table and stared at the flower in front of him, and then he called out so that Sarain could hear him say, "Wow, this flower is really lasting a long time! I wonder if it's a special kind of breed." "It must be," she replied as she entered the room, not wanting to go into much detail about the flower. "Seriously," Winston stated, "I don't think they usually last this long." "I wouldn't know…" Sarain started to say, and added, "I don't know much about flowers."

She then walked over to Winston, leaned down, and kissed him on the cheek, and said, "Okay, I won't be gone long, just need some sun and fresh air." "Do you want me to cook you something for when you get back?" he asked. Sarain then shook her head and said, "No, you shouldn't have to cook something when you're not even going to eat any of it." Winston nodded, and then took a hold of Sarain's hand before she had a chance to move away. He leaned in and softly kissed her hand, and muttered, "Come back to me soon." Sarain smiled, and replied, "Always," before she left out the door.

As Sarain trekked into town, she thought about the flower and wondered if she should hide it, or simply stop practicing her new found healing ability on it before Winston's curiosity peaked further. She knew that she needed to tell him about it, but she wasn't ready yet to open that box of mysteries, since she understood so little about it herself. But there was another reason she hesitated to tell him, and it was because she knew that he wouldn't like what she was doing to learn more about it.

Sarain lifted her head up as she ascended the stairs to the chapel, where David was waiting inside for her. She realized that she couldn't keep this a secret from Winston forever, and she knew that if he became aware of David, that he would likely be upset, and would want to meet him.

Once Sarain was inside the chapel, as usual, she chatted briefly with David first before they finally took time to pray. After which, David would have Sarain practice meditating, and focusing her thoughts. Once her mind was clear, he would have her focus on healing objects; a while ago he had started her out on plants, but now he had her healing small animals.

Sarain had confided in David about her healing ability just days after she had discovered it herself, and ever since she had been slipping out to visit and train with him every time she took one of her daytime walks away from Winston.

After her training, Sarain and David sat for a while outside on the chapel steps, talking once again. "I really wish you'd reconsider joining my people's mission; I know of a monastery not too far from here where monks are studying how to channel energy for the purpose of healing, much like yourself. If they had the use of your natural ability, I think it would save them years of study," David insisted. Sarain shook her head and stated, "I told you before, I can't leave Winston, not even temporarily; we just barely found each other again, I can't leave him now." "Well I really hope you reconsider, even if it's only for a visit; I'm sure they will make an exception so that Winston could join you," David pressed on, but Sarain knew that he would not be saying this if he knew that Winston was a vil sang. So she shook her head again, and replied, "That's not a possibility."

David sighed, and Sarain looked up at the sky, noting to herself where the sun was positioned. "I should be going," she stated. "Are you coming back tomorrow?" he asked. "I don't know yet," Sarain replied, and then added, "But I'll try to make it back soon." She stood up, and proceeded to descend the stairs when David called out behind her, saying, "I really think you found your calling." She stopped and glanced behind her, and at David, curiously. "Your ability; I think it's why you came back," he relayed. Sarain nodded her head lightly in agreement, but said nothing in response. She then continued down the steps, while thinking that if her healing abilities could bring her back from the dead, why couldn't they have done the same for her mother?

What made her ability different?

Sarain spent her walk home thinking about her mother, Ariana. She remembered how their clan had depended on her mother for healing; it was an ability that had been in their family bloodlines for generations, but it was also something that had skipped her grandfather, Delmar, the clan chief. Sarain had always thought that Delmar had been jealous of his daughter's ability, more than he was proud. And her father, Aion, had believed that it was Ariana's healing ability that had allowed her to bare him a child, Sarain.

Sarain was now beginning to believe that it was her new healing ability that brought her back from the dead, but how and why? It hadn't allowed Ariana to come back after Delmar poisoned her to death, and she had much more strength and control of her ability. Healing was new to Sarain, except for the fact that she had always healed quickly, but she had believed that that had been a part of her demonic side. Now she wondered if she had gotten her fast healing from her mother as well.

Sarain had so many questions, but there was no one she could ask; David knew only what he had learned from others who had the ability of channeling healing energy, but could not perform it himself. Sarain was curious if the monks at the monastery that David had spoken about might have answers for her, but she had no way of getting away from Winston long enough to go, nor did she want to part with him for such a length of time. They had spent so many years apart from one another, and had dealt with so many struggles to be together, that now that they were, Sarain didn't want to do anything that might ruin what they had together.

Sarain sighed with frustration as she stood outside Winston's house, took a deep breath, put on a smile, and opened the door to go inside.

As soon as Sarain stepped inside and closed the door, she was greeted by a smiling Winston. She looked at him curiously when she noticed that his smile was not his usual, and she asked, "What's going on?" Still smirking, Winston replied, "Why don't you go into the bedroom and find out." "Sounds kinky, but okay," Sarain remarked, and then began to walk down the hallway with

Winston following closely behind her. She pushed open the bedroom door to see candles lit around the room, rose petals spread on the bed, and on top of them, lay a sleek red dress.

"What's all this?" Sarain asked. Winston leaned in and whispered into her ear, "The dress is for tonight. I want to take you out; you deserve a real date. And the candles and roses are for afterwards." Sarain turned and looked up at him with amazement, "You didn't have to do all this. How'd you even pull it off? It's day time." Winston smiled again, and stated, "I've been sneaking the stuff in after my hunts the past few nights." She smiled up at him, and then grabbed onto his shirt and pulled him in for a kiss. When their lips parted, Sarain muttered, "You always did like me in red," and she kissed him again. Winston wrapped his arms around Sarain as her kisses started to become more passionate, and he struggled to say in between her kisses, "Maybe… the roses… and candles… can be for now." Sarain smiled as she kissed Winston once more, and then pushed him backwards onto the bed.

That night, Sarain dressed in the form-fitting gown. It was both sexy and elegant, but not something she was used to wearing. She wasn't used to getting fancy or girly, and not knowing what to do with her hair, she simply left it down to fall upon her shoulders.

When she stepped out of the bedroom to where Winston was waiting in the living room, she immediately saw his mouth gape open when his eyes settled upon her. She noticed that he had dressed up as well; he had pulled back his long blond hair into a tight braid and he was wearing a crisp white collared button up shirt with long sleeves and black slacks that appeared to be freshly pressed. These were just more new things that Sarain wondered where he could have hidden them. She thought about how handsome he looked; she hadn't seen him dressed up in such a way since she met him, back when he was working at the Purge, and it wasn't a time in which she had ever thought to appreciate his beauty.

"You look gorgeous," Winston stated as he walked towards Sarain. "Well you wanted this to be a real date, right?" she remarked. Winston smiled, and replied, "Yes, and I can't wait to show you off." "Where are we going, by the way?" she asked curiously. "That's a surprise," he replied.

It would take another half hour before Sarain would learn their destination, and that was when they finally arrived at it: a small, hidden building on the outskirts of Shaven. It wasn't until they stepped inside that Sarain realized that it was an Italian restaurant. As they waited for the hostess to seat them, Sarain whispered to Winston, "But you don't eat human food." "But you do, and I want you to enjoy a real meal for once," he whispered back, "I hear they have the best Italian food around."

The hostess came over and led them to a table in the center of a room much larger than Sarain had expected to see; the building had looked smaller from the outside, and she wondered if this was another magically shrouded place like the marketplace. Once they were seated and handed their menus, Sarain noticed, rather than looking at her menu, that a number of people were stealing glances at them, and that they were mostly men. Sarain leaned in towards Winston, and whispered, "People are staring at us." He smiled at her, and said, "Not us, dear. They are staring at you; I told you that you looked gorgeous." She blushed, and replied, "This can't be all because of me." "You always were one to avoid populated places; did you really think that all the attention you received was because of your former unique eye color?" Winston stated. Sarain's eyes scanned the room, and she realized that the men, almost all of them, and almost all of which appeared to be on dates, were stealing glances at her. Their eyes lingered all over her from her exposed legs, the curves of her dress, to the details of her face.

Sarain suddenly felt very vulnerable, noticeably so, that Winston leaned in and said, "Don't worry, you're leaving with me, and I'd never let anything hurt you." Sarain smiled, and soon ordered her food. Throughout the meal, Sarain ate her food, nervously, trying to avoid eye contact with any of the ogling men, while Winston simply sat back sipping a glass of red wine. It appeared that he had been truthful about wanting to show Sarain off, and as Winston sat there with an almost smug smirk on his face, it began to remind her of how he first stared at her when meeting her at the Purge, years before; like she was some sort of prize to be won. Sarain wasn't sure if she should be flattered or not, but she knew that Winston meant well, even if she happened to feel awkward by the gesture. When she was done eating, she quickly whispered to Winston, "Can we leave now?" "Are you not enjoying yourself?" he asked. "The food was great, this just isn't my sort of place," Sarain replied.

"Well, where would you like to go?" he asked.
"Somewhere where I'm not the center of everyone's
attention," she remarked with frustration. "That can be
done," Winston chuckled, and so he paid for their bill,
and they were quickly on their way.

Afterwards, Winston took Sarain on a walk, still
on the outskirts of town, in an area that she was
unfamiliar with. It was a clear night out with the stars
sparkling above, and a crescent moon's glow shining
down upon them. The area did indeed appear to be
deserted of people, allowing Sarain to no longer feel so
exposed, but she hadn't a clue where Winston was taking
her. He led her by the hand through what seemed like a
maze of back alleys, until finally they emerged out into
what looked to be a grand garden. High shaped hedges,
angelic statues, rose bushes, and fountains decorated the
area. It was like something out of a dream, and it seemed
very much out of place from the rest of that part of town.

Sarain gazed around in amazement, taking in the
beauty of their surroundings, and as she turned back to
Winston to comment on the place, she found him down
on one knee. He took her by the hand, smiled up at her,
and said, "Now I don't have a ring yet, but if you are
willing to be my wife, I will get you the most beautiful
ring that I can find." Sarain gasped with surprise, and
Winston continued to say, "I know that we haven't
actually been together long, but I don't need a lot of time
to know that I want to spend the rest of our lives
together… Sarain, will you marry me?"

A tear ran down her cheek, as she tried to catch
her breath. Sarain stared down into Winston's loving and

vibrant blue eyes, and knew she had to say, "I can't let you do that." "Why?" he asked more out of confusion than hurt feelings. "Because my life has an expiration date now," she answered and added, "I'm going to grow old, and some day I will die. I can't let you go through that." "That is something that I will have to deal with whether you're my wife or not, and it's something that I had already accepted the day I chose you over my old life working for Sephor," Winston told her.

Sarain took a deep breath, knowing that it was exactly this that she had always feared if she were to ever have a true relationship with Winston; that one day she would die, leaving him utterly heartbroken, and beyond repair. A tear escaped Winston's eye as he forced a smile and said, "You've already died once, as long as you promise to give me a few years before doing it again, then I'm good." Sarain laughed, and then gave him a sweet but almost sad smile. "Will you?" he asked again, this time sounding weak and a little helpless. She bit down softly on her lower lip for a moment, then lightly nodded her head, and softly answered, "Yes...yes, I'll be your wife."

A huge smile spread across Winston's face, and he quickly leapt up onto his feet. He wrapped his arms around Sarain, taking in her scent, and then stared down into her eyes for a moment before kissing her softly on the lips. Suddenly, and without warning, Winston scooped Sarain up into his arms, and gently spun her around, shouting, "She said yes!" as though wanting the whole world to know.

After a while of happily celebrating in the garden with dancing, and talk about their future, Sarain and Winston headed back home. Once they finally reached the dwelling's door, Winston playfully took Sarain into his arms again, wanting to carry her over the threshold. "Aren't you supposed to do this after we're married?" Sarain commented. Winston simply smiled, saying, "I can't wait that long."

She helped him open the door as he carried her inside, with the two of them giggling like children. But the game soon ended when they both saw someone standing inside their home. Winston immediately put Sarain down on her feet, as his expression turned gravely serious. She stared with confusion at the blond haired woman who stood in their living room. The woman looked oddly familiar, but Sarain couldn't place her, at first, until she noticed the way the woman stared adoringly at Winston. Suddenly it hit her where she knew this woman from; it was Alorea, from the Velvet Rose, the brothel that hid them from Sephor's men when they were out to kill them, and the same brothel that Winston once frequented before they met.

Sarain remembered Alorea always staring at Winston, longingly, and she remembered her even once telling her how lucky she thought Sarain was to have his affection. It was then that Sarain noticed how pale Alorea's complexion was, and the fact that even after over ten years, the woman looked exactly how Sarain remembered her to be. Sarain's gaze then went to Winston, and she saw the fear in his eyes as he waited for her to put the pieces together.

"Oh my god," Sarain began to say, "You turned her!"

Chapter 13

A look of disgust was on Sarain's face as she realized that Winston must have had a relationship with Alorea after she had left him years ago, a relationship that ultimately resulted in him turning her into a vil sang.

Winston stared at Sarain with dread, worried about how she would react, he pleaded, "This is not how it looks; she meant nothing to me." "But you turned her, didn't you?" Sarain asked, her voice shaking, and her anger growing. He hesitated to respond, but Sarain already knew the answer before he found the nerve to say, "Yes I did." A stern look came over Sarain's face as she glared back at Winston, and without another word, she turned and walked to the bedroom, slamming and locking the door behind her.

"What are you doing here?" Winston shouted, turning his attention to Alorea, "How did you find me?" Alorea stared off into the direction Sarain had left in, and ignoring Winston's questions, she remarked, "If I didn't know any better, I would have thought you turned her too; she doesn't appear to have aged, herself," Alorea turned and stared back at Winston, and added, "But then again, she smells so tastefully human. Is that your appeal to her?"

"Why in hell are you here?" Winston demanded with anger notably in his voice. "I'm here for you, silly," Alorea replied without worry over his tone. "Seriously? Even after the countless times I told you that I wanted nothing to do with you, and the years of abandonment?" Winston stated with annoyance. "Well evidently abandonment isn't that big of a deal with you either, if you're with 'her' again," Alorea slyly observed, and asked, "I thought she broke your heart?" "She is none of your business, nor am I," he firmly remarked. "Could it be that you're just trying to even the score with her? Use her for a blood companion for a while, and then break her heart like she broke yours?" she asked with hope and glee.

Winston gave Alorea a very stern and serious look as he replied, "I don't feed off of her." "And why is that? Is there something wrong with her?" she asked curiously. "No, she's just too good to be treated as my own personal blood bag," he said coldly to Alorea. "Oh… You mean like you did me," she stated with a sound of displeasure in her voice. "You need to get out," Winston said with hate. "But there's something I must discuss with you," Alorea pleaded. "Now!" he screamed at her. She stared over at him, looking a little hurt, but it was her determination that allowed her to say, "Perhaps this is a bad time; I'll return another night."

Alorea left with Winston bolting the door behind her. He then rushed to the bedroom door, worried about what Sarain must be thinking. He pounded on the door and called out, "Sarain please let me in!" "Is she gone?" he heard her ask from the other side of the door. "Yes," he simply said. The lock on the door clicked, but Sarain did not open the door. After a second to prepare himself, Winston turned the knob to open the door, gently pushed the door open, and inside he saw that Sarain had changed out of the gown he had given her and into the black attire she usually wore. The gown had been thrown and left on the floor, and the rose petals had been cleaned up and off the bed.

Sarain sat at the edge of the bed, staring off into space, as though contemplating her next move. Winston gazed at her with concern for both her and their relationship; he finally broke the awkward silence by asking, "Are you mad at me?" Without looking at him, Sarain replied, "Of course I'm mad at you." He walked over to her, and tried sitting next to her on the bed, causing Sarain to abruptly stand up. She angrily asked, "Were you in love with her? Is that why you did it?" "No," he quickly answered, "I never loved her. She was just 'there' after you left, that it seemed easy." "Then why?" she asked beginning to cry. "She begged me to turn her, and she had such a fascination with me that I thought she could help me get over you," Winston told her, feeling remorseful. "So it's my fault," she responded sounding hurt. "No!" he quickly replied moving towards her, "I thought it would be a good distraction; I had never turned anyone before…And I've not since!" "Then what happened?" Sarain asked finally looking Winston in the eye. "She became too obsessed with me, and it only worsened after I turned her. I couldn't stand it anymore, I finally left her and didn't look back," he explained, "I never thought I'd see her again; I don't know how she even managed to find me after all these years!" "Well she did!" Sarain shouted at him. "Please Sarain!" Winston began to beg, "Don't leave me over this! We both led different lives before we found each other again; this isn't a part of us!" "Maybe so, but you kept it a secret, and now I'm not sure if you're the person I thought you were," she stated. "You have always kept secrets from me!" Winston said furiously, and she didn't respond right away.

Sarain knew he was right, she was always keeping secrets from him, she was even now; and she was still reluctant to tell him about her healing ability. "You know I love you, Sarain," Winston said more calmly, "Please, still say you'll be my wife." Sarain gazed at Winston, wanting to say "yes" but finding herself instead saying, "I need to think about it." Winston looked hurt, but he sadly shook his head, and replied, "Okay." She then glanced at the bed and muttered, "I need to be alone tonight." He shook his head once more, and decided to take his leave, closing the bedroom door softly behind him.

Sarain sat back down on the bed, and let her head rest against the palms of her hands as she began to cry. Winston was sitting on the couch in the living room when he heard Sarain's sobs through the wall, and while his first thoughts were to go to her, he knew that she needed her space. He stretched out on the couch, and began waiting for sleep to find him, all the while wondering what lay in the future for him and Sarain.

Sarain woke the following morning after a long night of tossing and turning. She hadn't gotten much sleep, but she was tired of lying in bed. She wondered if Winston was awake and waiting for her outside her door. She wasn't ready to face him just yet, but she found herself needing to vent. She thought of David, and pondered if it was too early to go to the chapel to see him, but she decided to take the chance.

Sarain opened the bedroom door slowly, so as not to make it creak, and softly walked down the hallway, until finally she saw Winston asleep on the couch. It was just like how things had been before they got together, she thought, with him sleeping on the couch as she tried to sneak out. He appeared sound asleep, but his expression did not look peaceful; his hair and clothes looked tussled, as though he too had been tossing and turning.

A part of Sarain felt guilty for making Winston sleep on the couch, but she couldn't let him stay with her in bed like nothing was wrong. While she knew what went on between Winston and Alorea had nothing to do with her, Sarain still felt betrayed. She opened the door slightly; just enough to squeeze out and then gently shut it behind her.

Sarain hurried for the chapel, practically running the whole way, and she nearly tripped up the steps upon arriving, as she raced up them. She immediately found David sitting on a bench in the church's garden, and as soon as he noticed her, he put down the book that he had been reading.

"You're quite early for training," David commented at first, but when he got a good look at Sarain's composure, he asked, "Is everything alright?"

Sarain shook her head, and helplessly muttered, "No," before she finally began to cry. David let out a gasp of surprise from seeing Sarain's vulnerability, and he decided to do something out of character for him; he walked up to Sarain, and abruptly put his arms around her. This was an act that David usually avoided doing, not because the priesthood frowned upon it, but because something always seemed inappropriate whenever he thought about touching Sarain, as though it were forbidden.

Sarain quickly wrapped her arms around David's slender form, and sobbed against his shoulder. He stroked the back of her head softly, and whispered, "It'll be alright."

He held her for a while before Sarain finally calmed, and then he sat her down on the bench, where she finally managed to tell him what had happened. Sarain spoke of Alorea, a woman from Winston's past, suddenly showing up, and relayed to David that the two had shared a very intimate relationship that Winston had neglected to tell her about. Sarain made sure to leave out all parts that would have alerted David to them being vil sangs, but she had hoped that he would understand how very much she felt hurt and betrayed by such a secret.

"So are you afraid that he will leave you for this woman?" David asked. "No, I don't think he would," Sarain replied. "And you honestly believe that he is in love with you," he continued to question. "Yes," she stated softly. "Well, I understand why you feel betrayed, but if you both truly love each other, then you'll be able to work past this," David advised. Sarain nodded in agreement and muttered, "You're right."

David looked Sarain in the eye as he remarked, "You know though, if you feel you need time to contemplate things, than this could be the perfect time to take a trip to the monastery that I've been telling you about… I can accompany you as well, if you'd like." Sarain gave him a slight smile and replied, "No, that isn't necessary," then she wiped her eyes, and said, "I can't leave Winston, even with this." "Not even if it's a trip for reflection and contemplation?" David pressed. Sarain sighed, "He wouldn't understand."

David nodded, and after a moment of silence, he asked Sarain, "Well since you are already here, would you like to get in some training?" She smiled and replied, "Yes, I would like that very much."

They trained for hours, and much more intensely than usual. David got Sarain to clear her mind, and focus on healing once more, but this time he had finally become more physical in helping her channel her energy; often placing his hands on her shoulders, the top of her head, the back of her neck, and most frequently, holding her hands.

They sat on the ground, facing one another, as David held on to one of Sarain's hands, his other cradled the back of her free hand, and inside her palm lay the seed of a plant. He instructed her to close her eyes and focus her energy onto that seed, and while using his presence to stable her, he wanted her to make the seed grow. It was a different practice than they had ever studied; David had only instructed her before to heal and fix objects back to what they had already once been, and never before to make life grow.

Sarain wasn't sure if it was something that she could do, but as she felt David begin to gently squeeze her hand, she felt her nerves starting to calm, and she let go of her fears and doubts. She felt a cool breeze come over her, and while at first she thought it was a gust of wind, she soon realized that it was coming from her and the energy that was radiating off her. She opened her eyes to see what David had already seen, a small green vine had twisted out of the seed, and from that had sprung two small leaves.

Sarain smiled and gasped, as she proclaimed, "I did it!" "Yes you did," replied the seemingly proud David. She immediately placed the seedling on the ground, and quickly hugged the unsuspecting David. "Thank you so much," she said, "I could never have gotten this far without you!"

As Sarain began to pull away, she noticed a look upon David's face, a look of apprehension, and it was then that she realized that there was something she had overlooked throughout their training, and that was David's growing feelings for her. An awkwardness came over them, and it took Sarain a moment to realize the hour that it had become. They had spent so much time training that the sun was now beginning to set. She became flustered, saying, "I have to be getting back! Winston must be worried about me!" "I'm sure he is," David quickly stated, trying to brush off the awkwardness still, "You must hurry home before it gets much darker out."

Sarain thanked him once more, and they quickly parted ways. She began to race home, rushing through the darkened streets of Shaven, but it was already too late to make it back without worrying Winston. Night had already fallen upon her, and the moon had risen in the sky. Sarain knew that not only would Winston be furious about her staying out all day, but also being out at night would send him into an all-out panic. She took every shortcut she knew, and it wasn't until she reached the desert of Wormwood Alley that she finally stopped to catch her breath. She knew Winston's home was not far from there, and as she began to start her trek once again, she heard the snap of a twig from behind her.

Sarain quickly spun around; hoping at best to find Winston out looking for her, and at worse, Alorea, but what she did find surprised her completely. She found herself staring up at a tall male figure, whose golden eyes were very much fixated on her, while a smile spread across his pale face.

Chapter 14

"I've seen you before," Sarain stated while staring up at the man's sinister smiling face. "Yes, and I was hoping to see you again," the man with the golden eyes replied. "The marketplace…You tried to buy me," she said with disgust. "A wasted effort, I see, since I only had to wait to get you alone," he remarked. "I won't be going with you so easily," Sarain warned him. "I'd expect nothing less out of one as unique as you," he said smiling once more.

It was that instant that Sarain chose to run, racing towards the direction of Winston's house. "Winston!" she screamed, hoping by chance that she was close enough for him to hear her. Though soon she was tumbling towards the ground, as the tall man tackled her from behind. She let out a scream as she tried to kick the man off her; she clawed at his skin, and punched at his chest, but nothing seemed to deter him.

He grabbed her by the arm and began to drag her away, but Sarain twisted herself and broke free. She scrambled to her feet, and knowing that attempting to run again would prove useless, Sarain instead turned her attention to the man. She leapt at him, with her hands reaching for his eyes and tried to claw them out, but the tall man was too fast for Sarain now that she no longer had her own demonic speed. He grabbed her hands out of midair, and quickly struck her on the side of her head, knocking her unconscious. He picked up her limp body, placing her over one shoulder, and quickly sped away, running at a speed impressive even for a demon.

Winston paced the hallway, back and forth, waiting and worried about Sarain. She had already been gone when he awoke that morning, but noticing that her stuff was still there, he convinced himself that she had only went out on one of her walks. He knew that dusk was vastly approaching, and it was already later than when Sarain usually stayed out.

While pacing, Winston had seen that Sarain's ankh still lay under the sofa where she had dropped it weeks earlier. With their constant touching, Sarain hadn't bothered to think to wear it again. They had forgotten all about the pendant, and Winston's hope that by chance she would have worn it that day was dashed.

Once it became dark out, Winston only gave Sarain minutes with optimism that she would still come back on her own, but he was growing impatient, and finally decided to go look for her himself. As he headed for the door, he was immediately surprised to hear knocking come from behind it. He quickly opened it in hopes of finding Sarain standing on the other side, but was disappointed when he saw Alorea behind it instead.

"You don't look happy to see me," she said. "Do I ever?" he asked sarcastically. Alorea walked past him, pushing her way inside. "Is now a better time to talk?" she plainly asked. "Not really, I was about to go out and look for Sarain," Winston remarked. "Oh, did she leave you again?" Alorea crudely asked with a smile on her face. "No," Winston abruptly barked, "You forget that unlike you and I, she and I are actually in love!" "It didn't look that way last night," she replied. "Get out of here, Alorea! I'm too busy to deal with you right now," Winston said as he walked out the door.

He left Alorea behind and hurried his way into town, with his first destination being the marketplace. Once he arrived, he walked the alleyway back and forth, glancing over the venders and customers as he did so, but Sarain was nowhere in sight. He left the marketplace and walked down the streets of Shaven, quickly checking every darkened backstreet. Winston past stores and buildings that he didn't think Sarain would go into. He passed the deserted park that was even empty of wildlife, and headed for the only other place that he could think of that she would go to, the church.

Winston recalled following Sarain there once before, where he had seen her talking to a man on the front steps. Their interaction had made him jealous that day, but after Sarain had failed to ever bring the man up, he thought perhaps the interaction was innocent in nature. He wasn't sure what interest Sarain might have in the church, since he had always known her to be an atheist or at least agnostic in her behavior. Winston just hoped that Sarain would turn up soon.

He approached the chapel, and it loomed over him as it sat on top of a flight of stairs. Winston had avoided such buildings ever since he had been turned into a vil sang, and realized that crosses and other such holy relics burned his flesh. With a sigh of frustration, Winston proceeded up the stone steps. He passed a statue of the angel Michael, and headed for the chapel's large double doors, but he stopped for a second when he saw the large cross that hung above the doors. He knew it was likely just there to be symbolic, but in the town of Shaven, it could be meant as a deterrent for anything demonic. Winston shook his head; this didn't matter to him, he had to find Sarain, and so he pulled the doors open, and stepped inside the church.

The inside of the chapel was dark, only lit by candles. There was an altar at the front and wooden pews lined the center aisle. The chapel appeared to be empty except for one man, who was kneeling and praying when Winston stepped inside. The man turned around, and Winston right away recognized him as the man he had seen with Sarain weeks earlier.

"Can I help you?" David asked as he began to stand up. "Yes, I'm looking for a woman who may have been here. Her name is Sarain," Winston replied. "Oh yes, she was here, and left not too long ago," he said while walking towards him, "You must be Wins....ton," David spoke with his voice breaking as he stopped in his tracks. "She told you about me?" Winston curiously asked. "Yes, but evidently she left out a few things," David responded with his voice suddenly sounding tense. Winston noticed that David had begun glaring at him, so he asked, "What is it?" "You'd think an abomination, such as yourself, would know to stay out of a house of God," David firmly stated. "You know what I am, then," Winston remarked. "Yes, as a man of God, I've been trained to recognize your kind," David replied. "So you're a priest," Winston observed, "What exactly was Sarain doing here?" "If she wanted you to know, then I think she would have told you," David stated.

Winston felt his anger begin to rise, as detest for this priest grew; he may be a holy man, but Winston didn't trust him with Sarain. "Either way, I'm still looking for her," Winston stated. "Well if she shows up here again for one of her regular visits, then I'll tell her that you came looking," David acknowledged. Winston felt himself twitch when hearing the priest's words, and realized that Sarain had likely been visiting this man during her near daily walks. "Fine then," Winston stated. He turned to leave, and as he was walking out of the chapel, he heard the priest call out, "I would prefer if you didn't return here." The remark made Winston flinch with anger once again, but he didn't bother to reply; instead, he simply retreated down the steps and hoped that Sarain had arrived home by now.

Sarain opened her eyes to see that she was in a dark room, with her vision still slightly hazy from the blow that she had taken to her head. The walls of the room appeared to be made of stone, and the air was cold. Sarain's first thought was that she felt as though she was underground. She groaned as she shifted and realized that she wasn't even tied up, and then she soon saw why. She glanced up to see the tall man staring down at her with his golden eyes.

"Finally," he muttered, "You're awake." Sarain stared up at the odd looking man, knowing that he had to be some kind of demon as she asked, "Why am I here? Why didn't you just kill me?" The tall man looked at her with perplexity, "Why would I kill you? With energy like yours, it would be such a waste." Sarain continued to stare at the man with confusion, so he explained, "You're energy is like a flashlight, hell, a searchlight. Do you have any idea how rare that is?" Sarain still didn't appear to understand, and so the tall man bluntly said, "Someone like you is extremely coveted amongst my kind." "What are you going to do with me then?" she asked, "Feed off me?" The man's eyes went wide as he replied, "I wouldn't dare drink your blood!" Baffled again, Sarain stated, "Then what?" "Well I know a group that would be very interested in your existence... But they most likely will want to sacrifice you," the tall man answered.

Sarain shook her sore head with frustration, "So all this just to sell me off? Like some sort of dealer?" "Ya... Well, eventually..." he said, and then a smirk overcame his face, "But with that energy, and your beauty, I'm going to make sure to enjoy you first before I give you up." An appalled expression came over Sarain, as the tall man continued to say, "I may be a demon, but I'm still a man with desires, after all."

Sarain suddenly became frightened as she realized the man's intent, and she quickly began to scurry away as the tall man leapt toward her. He slammed down on top of her, pinning her to the ground with his weight. The tall man sloppily groped at her as he tried to flip her around to face him, but he was immediately met with Sarain scrapping her nails across his face, aiming for his eyes. He quickly closed his eyes to protect himself, but his left eye was just a fraction too slow to fend off Sarain's attack. She dug her nails in as deep as she could, tearing through the soft flesh and hitting against the side of his eye socket. The tall man screamed out in pain, his hands reaching for his eye, as he fell off Sarain.

She didn't waste any time. As soon as the demonic man was busy with the distraction of his searing pain, Sarain was on her feet, searching for the exit. The dwelling wasn't a complex one, but it was indeed underground. She appeared to be in some sort of modified drainage system, much like a sewer for excess rainwater, but it had been converted into this being's dwelling. Sarain ran down the damp and dark concrete passage towards where the only source of fresh air seemed to be coming. She pushed opened an iron gate-like door and raced out into the starry night. The demonic sounds of the man devilishly crying out echoed from the corridor behind her, as Sarain tried to locate where exactly in Shaven she was, and she realized that she was near the marketplace and not too far from Wormwood Alley and Winston's home.

Sarain ran as fast as she could, and soon realized that she was limping; she hadn't noticed the injury until now, but her left ankle was throbbing. She must have hurt it during her fight with the tall man earlier, when he had captured her. Sarain didn't dare to stop and check her wound since she had no idea if the tall man was chasing her or not. All she knew was that he had stopped screaming. She raced while wincing in pain, her heart beating rapidly as Winston's house finally came into view.

"Winston!" Sarain shouted, hoping that he would hear her as she sprinted for the door. When she reached it, she slammed her body against the door, and desperately tried its handle only to discover that the door was locked. "Winston!" she screamed again while pounding against the door, but it was a monstrous groan from behind her that would answer Sarain's pleas. She froze, speechless, and was afraid to turn around.

Chapter 15

Winston sighed as he approached his house and saw that the door was wide open, and he remembered that he had left Alorea alone in his house. Though this wasn't what he found upsetting, the truth was that he knew Sarain would have never left the door ajar, which led him to believe that she had not come home yet. As Winston stepped inside, everything looked in order, so he shut the door and locked it behind him, just in case Alorea decided to come back that night. Her words from earlier that evening rang out into his mind; "Did she leave you again?" It was something Winston didn't want to consider, but the fact was Sarain had left him once before. He felt fear begin to build in his gut as he looked towards the bedroom, and prepared himself to check for Sarain's things. Winston couldn't rule out the possibility that Sarain had come back and taken her stuff while he was gone, and with each step towards the bedroom, he felt himself growing more and more scared.

The bedroom door stood slightly ajar, but mostly closed, and as he approached it, he gently pushed the door open with the hinge squeaking as it swung. Winston's worried eyes searched the room, and he sighed when he saw Sarain's bag still sitting in the corner. Relief came over him as he thought that there was still a chance that Sarain was coming back, that perhaps she was merely taking time to clear her mind. It was then that Winston felt the tears on his chin, and he brought his hand up to wipe his face, realizing now that he had been crying.

Winston went into the bathroom and ran water in the sink. While the water ran, he cupped his hands and began splashing it on his face, cleaning away his tears and his frustration. He told himself to relax, and that Sarain would be coming back.

A sudden noise caused Winston to break from his concentration on calming himself down. He turned off the water and listened intently, trying to figure out what it was that he had heard before. The air was silent, and Winston began to lean back down to the water in the sink when the sound of rapid pounding came against the door. He flinched, being caught off guard by the noise, but it was what came next that scared him; the sound of Sarain screaming out his name in fear.

Winston hurried to the door with panic, not knowing what it was that he was going to find behind it. He fumbled with the lock for a moment and as soon as he opened the door he found himself falling back. Winston groaned from the ground as he looked up to see what had happened, and he noticed that Sarain was lying on top of him. It took only a split second for him to see the bloody claws marks going down her back, and his eyes quickly located the source of her injury. Winston saw the tall man standing in the doorway with one golden eye ablaze.

"You!" Winston shouted, immediately
recognizing the man as the one who tried to buy Sarain
weeks earlier, despite the fact that the man now appeared
to have one of his eyes clawed out.

Winston quickly sprung onto his feet, and flew at
the demonic man, who lunged right back at Winston. The
two men collided into the living room, crashing onto the
floor. The man swung at Winston with a clawed hand that
looked like the man's nails had retracted out like a cat's.
The tall man narrowly missed scraping Winston's face
but hit his shoulder, and though the man's nails left a
bloody claw mark on Winston's skin, he did not react.
Instead, his blue eyes burned furiously as he knocked the
demonic man off of him. Winston's glowing eyes then
noticed something on the ground that the tall man hadn't
seen, Sarain's ankh. Winston quickly grabbed the holy
relic and leapt onto the villain, who hissed at the sight of
the ankh. Winston forcibly shoved the ankh down into the
tall man's open mouth, and the demon began to gag as he
choked on the pendant. Dark blood gurgled out the
creature's mouth, but this was not enough to appease
Winston. He stood up and proceeded to kick the intruder
in his stomach, with each thrust being more and more
powerful. The snap of bones could be heard as Winston
stomped on the man, and when the demon failed to move
any longer, Winston leaned down and stared at its lifeless
face, and then grabbed a hold of his head and yanked.
The tall man's head came ripping off with dark blood
spraying across the room. Now satisfied that the man was
dead, Winston threw the demon's head out the door, and
then he bent down over the body once again. This time
Winston scooped up something from the bloody mess,

and when he stood up, he heard a weak gasp that caught his attention.

Winston looked down towards the ground, and slightly behind the sofa, he saw a weak Sarain huddled and staring up at him in shock. Her eyes were fixated on the object he held in his hand, a chain, and at the end of that chain was her pendant, with the now filthy ankh gently resting against Winston's skin; his unburned skin.

"What the he…" Sarain begin to say, and then stopped as her eyes immediately rolled back into her head, and she slumped to the ground. Winston dropped the ankh and quickly rushed to Sarain's side. He hadn't thought that Sarain's wounds were that bad, he had certainly seen her receive worse in her time, but now that she was mortal, perhaps she couldn't deal with as much pain.

Winston scooped her up into his arms and carried her out of the bloody mess of a room.

Sarain woke about an hour later feeling disoriented, and it took her a minute to remember what had happened. She recalled seeing Winston not get burned by her ankh, and she wondered for a moment if she had been a bit delirious before she had passed out, wondering if perhaps she could have been mistaken about what she had seen.

Sarain groaned as she began to sit up, and the pain from the claw marks on her back went shooting throughout her body. She let out a short yelp, and lay back down on her side instead. Soon, the door cracked open, and Sarain saw Winston's blue eyes peeking in at her. "Are you okay?" he asked, pushing the door open. "Yeah, I'm just sore," Sarain replied. They were silent for a while, with an awkwardness still between them. "The den is mostly clean," Winston finally said, "But there is yet another blood stain that I can't get up off of the floor.....At least it's not my blood this time." Sarain nodded, but didn't reply to Winston's remark, so he took that as a cue that she wanted to be alone, and he said, "I'm sure you want your rest, so I'll leave you be."

"Wait," Sarain muttered. "Did you need something?" he asked. She stared up at him from the bed, looking exhausted, as she spoke, "I know things are still weird right now between us, and I can't promise that things will go back to the way they were. But I really don't want to be alone right now." "What do you want me to do?" Winston quickly replied. "Hold me," she said.

Winston walked over and lay down next to Sarain, who immediately snuggled up next to him. He gently placed his arm around her, making sure not to disturb her injury, and held her as he always had during the days they slept together. In minutes, Sarain's breathing softened, and Winston knew that she had fallen asleep, but he lay there awake, cherishing the moment as he worried that once Sarain was well again, she would no longer want him by her side. He held on to her as though it may be the last time, and a part of him knew that they both were changing.

What would become of them was a mystery.

Sarain awoke late the next day to find Winston already awake and watching over her. His blue eyes lingered on her, and she gave him a soft smile as she said, "I thought you'd still be sleeping." "I don't need as much sleep as you've needed lately, besides, it's almost evening," Winston remarked. "Oh wow, I slept the day away….. Have I been sleeping more?" Sarain asked. "For about a week or so," he relayed, "Haven't you noticed?" She thought about it, and realized she had been falling asleep earlier lately, and sleeping in more at times. "Have you been feeling okay lately? I know you must be sore from last night, but other than that, has anything else been bothering you physically?" Winston asked curiously. Sarain thought of all the energy she had been using lately while training with David and healing various objects. She wondered if she should tell him what she had been up, and she found herself starting to say, "Actually, there is something…"

Suddenly, Sarain's stomach growled loudly, and Winston immediately sprung up and said, "Oh you must be starved! You didn't eat last night. Let me get you something from the kitchen," and with that, Winston was gone. Sarain sighed; she had had so much trouble working up the courage to tell Winston about her healing ability, that this seemed almost like fate. She sat up in bed, and waited for him to return. As she waited, she thought again about the events of the night before, and recalled how it appeared as though her ankh no longer affected Winston, and she wondered if he was keeping a secret from her as well. She contemplated whether or not to ask him as much, but she knew that things were barely starting to calm down between the two of them, and bringing up such a subject involving further secrets may only drive a bigger wedge between them.

After a few minutes, Winston returned with a bowl of fruit that he handed to an, indeed, hungry Sarain. She immediately picked up an apple and bit into it, and as she leaned forward over the bowl of food, Winston gazed at the clawed up, blood stained shirt on her back. "Maybe you should change out of that shirt, and I should probably dress your wound for you... How does it feel by the way?" Winston commented. "The stinging has stopped," Sarain replied with a mouth full of food. "That's good, it's probably not infected then," he stated. Winston subsequently left the room for a moment, and quickly returned with a bowl of water, a rag, and some antiseptic. He placed a clean shirt next to Sarain, who put down the bowl of fruit, and began to lift her shirt.

"This feels familiar," Sarain stated, as Winston pressed the wet rag to her back. "I know what you mean; I always have to tend to your wounds. You know, you really need to be more careful," Winston replied. Sarain wasn't sure if he was feeling the same nostalgia that she was, as she thought of the first time they had made love so many years ago, after he had cleaned her wounds from a battle. "You shouldn't have been out so late," he stated. "I know, I lost track of time," she remarked. "You mean while you were with that priest," Winston commented.

Sarain suddenly stiffened as she asked, "You know about David?" "Yeah... I talked to him yesterday while I was out looking for you," Winston replied. Sarain found this odd, and so she asked, "Why did you think to check the chapel?" It was that moment that Winston realized that he had said too much, and Sarain immediately asked, "Have you been following me?" Winston hesitated to answer, and Sarain took that as guilt. She quickly turned around and remarked, "You tell me to be more careful, and clearly you're sneaking around during the day, or does the daylight not affect you anymore like my ankh?" "That's not true," Winston immediately replied. "Which part?" she asked, and added, "Because I saw you holding my ankh last night and I don't see any burn marks on your hands!" "Great, turn this around on me, when you're the one who's been keeping secrets!" Winston barked. "My secrets never hurt anyone, or do I have to remind you about your friend, Alorea!" Sarain shouted. Winston groaned with frustration as he ignored her accusation and instead pointed out, "So you admit that you're keeping secrets from me!" "Yeah...well it looks like I have good reason to," she shot back. Winston stood up, and while throwing the damp rag down, said, "Well maybe I do too! And by the way, you wounds are completely gone; just a bunch of clean skin under all that caked on blood, so how about you explain that one to me, or is that just another one of your secrets?" He stormed off before getting his answer, leaving Sarain stunned, not only from the sudden argument, but surprised as well by the fact that she had healed so quickly. She hadn't done such a thing since her days of having demon blood coursing through her veins, which she no longer felt, but now, the only thing that could possibly allow her to heal so quickly would be her ability to heal things. But she hadn't realized that her body would heal itself without her focusing her energy first.

And she wondered just how much her healing power was capable of.

Chapter 16

After about ten minutes of arguing with herself in her head, Sarain finally decided to come clean with Winston about everything, and hoped that afterwards he would do the same. She hesitantly left the bedroom and slowly walked down the hallway only to find the living room empty; Winston had gone out. Sarain sighed, not knowing whether Winston had left in anger or simply just to hunt. She sat down on the sofa, and began to wonder how long Winston would be gone.

As Sarain waited, she gazed down to see the blood stain left by the tall man the night before, and decided that she no longer wanted to sit there so close to such a fresh and gruesome memory. She got up from the sofa and walked over to the kitchen table where she saw her ankh, cleaned and laying on the table.

"Well that answers that question," Sarain said to herself, referring to whether or not it affected Winston anymore. She picked up her pendant, and decided that even though Winston's immunity to it brought up so many questions, at least it meant that she was safe to wear it around him. Sarain knew now more than ever that she needed to be more careful now that she was mortal, and clearly a target amongst the demon kind. She would, from this moment on, have to rely on her ankh and her basic fighting skills to protect her, much like she had to do as a child when she was living on the streets.

No sooner than she had clasped the chain around her neck, did a knock pound against the door. Sarain stood up and moved towards the door, hoping that it would be Winston standing on the other side having decided to come back home, but she knew that Winston likely wouldn't have knocked, so she took caution as she open the door, and to her disappointment stood Alorea on the other side. Alorea also appeared disappointed by the sight of Sarain, and quickly verbalized it by saying, "Oh, it's you. I guess you came back after all."

"Why are you here?" asked an annoyed Sarain. "I'm here to see Winston, and perhaps talk him out of wasting his time on you," Alorea smugly replied. "He's not here, so you can go find someone else to pathetically throw yourself at," Sarain stated, and began to close the door on her when Alorea immediately stopped it and said, "You know, I'm sensing that you're not as high and mighty as you were when we first met. In fact, there is definitely something different about you...something much more vulnerable." "You are mistaken," Sarain quickly shot back, and tried once again to slam the door shut, but this time Alorea grabbed her by the arm. Sarain tugged her arm away with a scowl, and with that motion, her ankh came bouncing out from underneath her shirt. Alorea's glowing eyes immediately focused on the relic, and she quickly let go of Sarain and growled. Sarain took this opportunity to finally slam the door in Alorea's face and lock it shut.

Sarain sighed, both out of relief and frustration; once upon a time, Alorea was the type of vil sang that Sarain could kill like swatting a fly; but now, any demonic creature posed a threat to her. She began to wonder if any amount of combat training would allow her to be even half the hunter she used to be. Sarain groaned when she realized that she was longing for the days that demon blood powered her own veins, and headed back to the sofa, no longer caring that it was stained with blood. There she decided to wait no matter how long it took Winston to come home.

A few hours later, Sarain awoke to the sound of the door creaking open; she had accidentally fallen asleep out of boredom, while waiting for Winston. She lifted her head up, and slowly got up from her position on the couch to see Winston walking through the door.

"Where have you been?" she sleepily groaned. "I was out hunting," he responded shortly. "For that long?" she questioned. "Wildlife doesn't just walk up to you and say, 'Eat me'," he sarcastically stated. "Well you could have told me, you didn't have to leave without a word like that," Sarain argued. "At least I didn't take ten years to return," Winston shot back.

Sarain paused with surprise from Winston's harshness, and finally mustered up saying, "That's not fair." "And you judging me for things in my past aren't fair either," he remarked. "This whole ankh thing isn't in your past, but speaking of past mistakes, Alorea came here looking for you again," she announced. Winston immediately glanced Sarain up and down and he asked,

"Did she try anything with you?" "I didn't give her the chance," Sarain replied. "Good, though maybe you should stop answering the door," he stated. "I'm not a child," she immediately said, and continued, "And you really need to clean up this mess you made with her. I don't like her coming around... Unless you do." "What's that supposed to mean?" Winston defensively asked. "Exactly as it sounds," Sarain bickered, "You did frequent her brothel after all; that doesn't sound like a man who's into monogamy."

Winston groaned with frustration as he rolled his eyes and said, "Really? After everything we've been through, you think so little of me?" "I'm just not sure I really know you anymore," Sarain muttered. "God, Sarain! You know you're the only woman I've ever loved! Seriously, how many times do I have to risk my life to prove it to you?" Winston shouted. Sarain did not reply, instead she glanced away with a guilty look upon her face. Winston sighed with annoyance, and then to Sarain's surprise, Winston was suddenly standing in front of her, having used his demonic speed. He put his hand on the back of her neck and pulled her to him for a kiss.

Winston kissed Sarain hard, while pressing her against him. He kissed her hungrily, as though arguing with her had aroused him. Sarain, on the other hand, did not share his enthusiasm, and as she kissed him, became disgusted when a metallic taste that could only be blood, lingered on Winston's lips. She pushed him away, and quickly complained, "I can still taste the blood on you!" "What do you expect?" Winston bellowed, "I'm a vil sang, after all!" "Ya, well I'm not, and I have no love for tasting blood!" Sarain yelled.

Sarain turned to leave when Winston immediately grabbed her, and began kissing her again. His hands ran over her body, as she struggled with him. Sarain quickly stomped on Winston's foot, which abruptly stopped him long enough for Sarain to shove him away, and slap him across his face. "See! I don't know you anymore!" Sarain screamed at him, and stormed off to the bedroom where she slammed and locked the door, leaving Winston all alone.

He stood there in shock, not by the fact that Sarain had fought him off, but stunned by his own actions. Winston remained motionless, wondering what had come over him, and why he hadn't been able to control himself.

"What's happening to me?" Winston whispered to himself.

Chapter 17

Early the next morning, Sarain found herself on the way to the chapel; once again, having snuck out of the house while Winston was fast asleep on the couch. Sarain had wished to be able to talk to David sooner, but with Alorea and other demons lurking around at night, she knew it wasn't safe, and she knew that Winston would be against it at any hour. But Sarain didn't care what Winston thought of her visits to see David, because she knew that they were innocent in nature, and it was the nature of Winston's actions that she was beginning to doubt.

Sarain hurried through the streets of Shaven, oblivious to all who were out enjoying the day. She had not cared to watch the kids playing in the park, or the lovers who walked hand in hand. She paid no attention to the wildlife that scurried around her or the birds that sang their morning songs. Her sole concern was seeing the priest who seemed to have answers to all her questions, hoping that he would help her with the cloud of frustration that lingered in her mind.

Sarain ran up the stone steps, past the angel statue, and went for the chapel's double doors. And as she opened the doors, she quickly saw that, for once, there was a mass in session. Sarain had never made it there early enough on a day that they held them, but saw that the church was nearly full with parishioners, and up at the podium stood David, who was officiating a sermon.

David stood there for a moment, surprised to see Sarain, who was now taking a seat in the back of the chapel, but finally found his train of thought once again as he spoke, "The Bible tells us to abide by faith, hope, and love; but that of these three, love is the greatest. For it was love for the world that God gave his one and only son...And it tells us that love is patient, and love is kind. It protects, it trusts, it hopes, and always perseveres," and then he gazed over at Sarain as he said, "Love never fails."

Sarain wondered if David meant for her to hear the passage in particular, wondering if it was meant for her to remember when it came to her problems with Winston. She listened intently, as David continued his sermon, preaching more of love and God's ways, with him periodically glancing in her direction. In fact, he mostly only gazed at her when he spoke, so much so, that it seemed as though he were only talking to her.

Finally David began to wrap up his sermon, and after he blessed the congregation, everyone started to disperse. Most of the flock left, with only a few that lingered behind to have a word with Father David. Sarain waited patiently as the remaining parishioners talked to David, telling him stories, and asking his advice. One older woman even told him that if only he weren't a priest that she would fix him up with her daughter, and it was a comment that seemed to make David uncomfortable.

As Sarain watched and waited, she began to wonder how many people the young priest instructed such as herself. She watched him relay stories to a few, a soft smile upon his face, and she saw that he still stole the occasional glance toward her direction, as though letting her know that he hadn't forgotten about her.

Once the final person left through the chapel's double doors, David's soft smile immediately changed into a look of concern as he turned to Sarain. "You're okay!" he said with distress, "I was so worried when that creature came here looking for you!" "Oh," Sarain replied with shock, "You know what Winston is?" "I am no fool, Sarain; I can recognize a demon when I see one. I just thought that you had better judgment than that," David relayed. "It's not as simple as all that, I've known Winston for years, and he's always been loyal and trustworthy to me… It's just, he's changed recently," Sarain explained. "Demons are great at manipulating," he began to say, but Sarain quickly cut him off by saying, "You don't understand." "Oh Sarain, you're the one who doesn't understand how the mind of a demon works," David abruptly jumped back in, but Sarain cut him off once more, and this time she left him speechless when she said, "But I do, because I was a demon!"

David stood there in disbelief as Sarain explained, "I was born with demonic blood inside me. In fact, I became a full-fledged vil sang right before the sun killed me… I wasn't lying when I told you that I believed that I had come back from the dead, but when I came back, I had become more human than I have ever been before!" "You can't be serious?" David said with skepticism, "Such a thing isn't possible." "My mortal mother bore my demonic father a child, and people thought that wasn't possible. I have had many demons try to possess me like I was some sort of grand prize; even as recently as the night that you saw me last, when a demon that saw me once before followed me home and abducted me," she relayed. David gave her a look of shock as he asked, "Are you alright?" "I'm fine. I fought him off, and made it back home where Winston destroyed the monster. And that is what I've been trying to explain to you about Winston, he's not like the demons you know of," Sarain remarked. "Then why have you been doubting him?" David asked curiously. "Because since I've been back, he's been changing," she replied. "Well, I imagine having you die and then returning from the dead, could do a number on a loved one's psyche," he commented. "But not all his changes are to his personality…He's also changing physically… I've seen him hold a holy relic and not get burned," she stated.

David took this with concern, and then took a moment to think before he remarked, "Actually, I was surprised that he was able to walk in here without any sign of affliction… Perhaps you should tell me all you know about him." And Sarain did exactly that.

Over the next few hours, Sarain told David everything, and not just about Winston. She told David about how they met, how Winston had saved her, and fought by her side numerous times, but she also told him about her own obstacles. She told him about the massacre of her clan, and the countless people she had lost. She told him about her struggles with the demonic blood, and about her obsessive father.

By the end of her story, David was hanging on her every word with amazement, until finally she finished and he said, "How have you managed to make it through all that?" Sarain let out a soft chuckle as she said, "I didn't. I died. I just got lucky that I somehow managed to come back." "Yes, and it was by the grace of God that you returned," David spoke, "And surely your healing ability is the tool he used to get you here." "I guess," Sarain said sounding uncertain, "But I don't know why I'm back, or what I'm supposed to be doing. Yes, I can heal things, but I don't know what for." "It sounds like you need a flock, much like your mother was a healer for your clan," David theorized. "But what of Winston?" Sarain asked. "Winston got you to where you needed to be, but if he is changing like you said, then perhaps he is no longer the person you need," he remarked. "I don't think I'm ready to leave him…I'm not sure if I even can," Sarain spoke truthfully. "And I don't want you to leave the safety of this chapel, Sarain, but some things just aren't within our power to control. It's simple, if he is becoming dangerous, then you shouldn't stay with him," David stated.

Sarain sighed as David's worried eyes gazed upon her. "Give me time, I can't just give up on him after the first obstacle that is thrown our way; I did that once before, and I've regretted it ever since," she told her friend. David closed his eyes for a moment, and took a deep breath before saying, "Be careful, Sarain, the path you're walking down is a hazardous one, and you've been blessed once already with a second chance; I doubt another will be in your future."

Sarain left the church with David's words weighing heavy on her. She began to take her usual short cut through the alleyway across from the chapel, when something caught her attention – a cloaked figure waiting in the darkened alley. Sarain stopped in her tracks, and almost turned around until she saw the twin blue glowing lights from inside the head of the cloak. "Winston," Sarain muttered.

He began to leave and Sarain immediately chased after him, "Winston," she called out, and he stopped. He turned around and Sarain could see that he was angry. "You came out like this to come looking for me? You know how dangerous that is?" Sarain anxiously asked. "It's no worse than you going out alone after what happened the other night!" Winston shot back, and added, "Did you learn anything from that?" "I wasn't going to lose track of time again, I was already heading home!" Sarain replied. "It doesn't matter, what does is that you snuck out again! And you came here to see him!" Winston shouted. Sarain sighed, and tried to explain, "It's not like that, he's my friend, that's it!" "But why do you need him?" Winston begged, "Why is he so important? Why can't I just be enough for you?"

Sarain felt her eyes begin to well up when she heard Winston's voice break, and saw tears fall from his eyes. "Winston, I love you, but... I'm human now and I'm going through something that you just can't understand. I have to live my life; I can't stay confined in that house day and night. I can't be kept like a prisoner." Winston winced with Sarain's words, and he weakly spoke, "That's how you see your life with me? As a prisoner?" "It's how you've been treating me lately," Sarain replied. "Well, if life with me is so awful, then I'll just leave," he snapped at her. "Winston," she said distressingly, "That's not what I meant; I just want things to be how they were, when you trusted my judgment and capability to take care of myself." "But you can't!" Winston shouted, "You always get into trouble, and now you're not even strong enough to fight back!"

Sarain began to cry. She hadn't realized just how much faith he had lost in her. When seeing her reaction, Winston immediately said, "See, I can't do anything right. You're better off without me...Maybe you should be with 'him'," and he turned to leave. "Wait," Sarain quickly said, but it was of no use; Winston had sped away, using his demonic speed.

Sarain stood there alone, not knowing where Winston had gone, or if he was coming back.

Chapter 18

Night had finally fallen, and Winston found himself loitering in the garden where he had proposed to Sarain. He thought of how happy they were that night, and how Sarain had accepted his marriage proposal. Then he thought of how she had hesitated at first, not because she didn't love him, but because she worried that their lives would no longer fit together now that she was human. Winston began to wonder if Sarain was right, and perhaps they were wrong for each other. He loved her so much, but his love only seemed to be holding her back now; he was no longer needed to help her fight, because she was no longer strong enough to fight. Sarain had already completed her lifelong mission, and all that was left now was for her to live her life; but with Winston's limitations as a creature of the night, he knew that he couldn't give her the full life that she deserved. He couldn't give her a nice house with a white picket fence, he couldn't grow old with her, and they couldn't have a family together.

Winston sighed, knowing that he and Sarain were growing apart; their lives were leading them in different directions, and he knew that the true and logical choice would be to let her go. But could he?

It was that moment, when a breeze blew softly, that Winston suddenly noticed a familiar scent lingering nearby. His body tensed as he muttered, "You can stop hiding, I know you're there." A pale and slender figure then stepped out from behind the high hedges, and walked towards the disheartened Winston. "How did you find me?" he asked solemnly. "I got lucky to be passing by; I'd recognize your scent anywhere," Alorea softly replied. Winston groaned, but didn't comment further. Alorea began to look him up and down with her eyes, after which she said, "You know, you shouldn't be with someone who causes you so much pain and grief... Love should be easy." "What would you know of love?" Winston stated, "Real love is reciprocated, all you know is infatuation." "I know that I would do anything for you, and I know that I'm here and she isn't, so how is your love really reciprocated?" Alorea remarked.

Winston ignored the comment, and continued trying to keep to his thoughts of Sarain, and how to deal with their problems. Alorea stood there for a while, simply watching him, while he tried to shut her out. After a few minutes of silence, Alorea took a few steps closer to Winston as she said, "I have always dreamed that you would one day look at me the way you look at her." Winston sighed, but still didn't say a word. Alorea moved nearer to him, bringing her lips up towards his ear as she whispered, "It could be so easy with me... If you just let me in, you could love me too."

Alorea reached her hand up to Winston's cheek, and softly caressed it. She let out a somewhat erotic sigh of relief, as though she had been desperately longing to touch him. With her mouth still near Winston's ear,

Alorea leaned in further until her lips grazed against his other cheek. A part of Winston shuttered, and he wasn't sure if it was out of disgust or arousal. He remained motionless, and Alorea took this as consent to continue; she lightly slid her lips across his cheek until she neared his mouth, then she slowly raised herself up until her upper lip began to touch his lower. They softly and just barely touched, and Alorea began to stretch up further when Winston suddenly took a hold of her by her shoulders and forcefully shoved her away. She fell back hard, landing on her tailbone, and wincing from pain that wasn't all physical.

Winston sneered at her as he said, "Like you could ever replace her; you don't even compare to Sarain." Alorea scowled as she angrily asked, "If you love her so much, then why are you keeping the truth from her?" "What are you talking about?" the confused Winston replied. "I'm 'talking about' what you've been doing to this town!" she shouted, "Or did you think no one would notice?" Winston then shot Alorea a puzzled look as he questioned, "Exactly how long have you been in town?" "Long enough to know where the real power is here," she answered coarsely. "What are you talking about? Any real power here has been dead for over a year now," he remarked. "You mean when you and your girlfriend went after the Brotherhood?" Alorea noted. "Who have you been talking to?" Winston immediately asked. She rolled her eyes and replied, "Come on, do I really need to answer that? You know you didn't kill the whole Brotherhood; you guys were too busy getting revenge against her father. You let like half of them run away!" "So that's who you've been talking to, the

Brotherhood? Is that how you knew where to find me?"
Winston pried.

Alorea began to get up; she dusted herself off, and
then finally replied, "They came looking for me recently.
It seems that you caught their eye, and they wanted to
know all about you." "Why are they so interested in me?
If they want revenge, why not just simply kill me?" he
asked. "They don't want you dead, silly," she said with a
smile, "They want you to be their new leader." "What!
Why on Earth would they want that after I helped take
down their last leader?" he said appalled. "Because they
can sense the power growing inside you," Alorea
answered, "And they think that you could wield the
power of an Ancient some day."

"That's crazy," Winston stated, and started to
walk away when Alorea called out, "Don't tell me that
you haven't noticed the changes!" He stopped for a
moment and glanced back at her as she said, "Your
energy; even I can tell it from here, that it's grown
immensely. Power like that has got to have been taking a
toll on your body; I imagine it's only a matter of time
before your body starts making adjustments to handle
it… If it hasn't already."

Winston turned away from Alorea without a word
and he proceeded to walk away, no longer wanting to
hear any more of what she had to say.

Sarain wandered through town, looking for
Winston, and knowing that he would be furious if he
knew that she was out at night, alone, and unarmed with

only her ankh to aide her. But she had to find him, she couldn't leave things with how their fight had ended, and he hadn't returned home. She worried that Winston had done something crazy and impulsive while he was out during the day, and now she was desperately looking for any sign of him.

Sarain's first thought was to check the marketplace; it was the site of their reunion after all, and it was a place that a vil sang, such as Winston, could mingle in without feeling out of place. Though the same could not be said about Sarain. She noticed now that many of the alley's occupants gazed at her, some sneaking quick glances, while others flat out stared. Sarain wasn't sure if this was a result of the supernatural kind recognizing her as the hunter she once was, or if it was the energy coming off her that the tall man told her about when he claimed that she was like a spotlight to his kind.

Sarain tried to ignore the gawks, but had trouble doing so, as some of the creatures looked at her as though she were a shiny new toy. Others gazed at her in confusion or disbelief, and there were even a few that stared at her with fear.

Only half of the people, if you could call them that, looked human; most were humanoid, and clearly part demonic, but still these odd looking creatures found Sarain to be the strange one. It bothered her that she didn't know what these beings were thinking, but since none of them made an attempt to hassle her, Sarain knew it best not to press the issue. Besides, she had to find Winston, and after having paced the alley back and forth, three times, she knew that it was time to try somewhere else.

Sarain's next stop was the park, though only because it was the nearest location to her that she thought Winston might go. But as she arrived to the broken down place she found only a small group of teenagers there, drinking; five kids in total, three male and two female. Sarain began to walk away when she heard one of the boys call out, "Hey you! Come over and join us!" she then heard the other boys mutter about her being "hot" while the girls seemed to complain and state that she looked "too old" for them. One of the boys then remarked that he didn't care about age, while Sarain continued to walk away. After a moment she heard the sound of one of the boys getting up and starting to jog towards her. Sarain didn't bother to look back as she continued walking, but tensed up her body. The young man tapped Sarain on the shoulder and she quickly spun around.

"Whoa," the boy immediately reacted, "I just wanted to know if you wanted to hang with us?" Sarain glared at the intoxicated teenager, shaking her head and muttering, "No." She turned back around and headed away, quickening her pace, while the same boy called out, "Could you buy us some beer?"

Sarain hurried away from the park, more annoyed than scared by the teenage boy who had now returned to his group. Sarain never could understand the ways of what was viewed as "normal" people, especially teenagers. She couldn't see the appeal of sitting around in the dark and getting drunk; instead all she could think of was how easy of targets those kids made to a hungry demon that might be lurking nearby.

It was then that Sarain thought of the next place she wanted to check for Winston, in the seedy part of Shaven. She thought of how she herself had hit the dive bar district when she was feeling lost the year before, and Winston had found her and brought her home. She wondered if Winston could be doing the same and trying to lose himself in alcohol.

The seedy part of Shaven likely wasn't the best or safest place for Sarain to be, but it wasn't demons that she had to worry about there, just good old fashion human crime. Still, it would have been better if Sarain had been carrying a weapon, especially since her ankh would have no effect on mortals, but she didn't want to turn back now. She had to find Winston.

Downtown Shaven consisted of a few rundown bars, a strip club, and a couple of pawnshops. This part of town wasn't as deserted as everywhere else; there, outside the bars, lingered drunks, patrons, and a few questionable women who were likely prostitutes. Other than the marketplace, this was the most life that Sarain had seen around town that night. Neon lights flickered, and the smell of stale smoke and vomit lingered on the streets. Sarain made her way to the first bar, which was dimly lit. Upon entering, Sarain immediately caught the eye of a few male patrons, but these looks were not like the ones she had received at the marketplace, these men's thoughts were obvious with their lustful gazes. Sarain wasn't even wearing anything revealing, but with the lack of women in that bar, she wasn't surprised that the drunken men would ogle her so.

It didn't take Sarain long to realize that Winston wasn't there; it didn't feel like a place that he would be; it was too desperate. She moved on to the next bar, which appeared to be a place that the more college-aged people frequented. It was a lot more crowded than the last place, with some of its customers dancing on a small dance floor in back. The women there were dressed scantily, with the men eager to acknowledge this. Everyone seemed a lot happier and excited than the depressing atmosphere of the last bar, but this didn't appear to be a place Winston would frequent either, and he was nowhere in sight.

Sarain walked out, and then gazed across the street where another bar stood, and next to it, the strip club. Sarain contemplated which to try next; she didn't lavish the thought of going into a strip club especially with the kind of people it catered to, but then she thought of the places Winston frequented when they first met. She knew she had to at least take a quick glance inside the strip club if she truly wanted to find Winston, because if he was trying to hide from her, then that would be the place to hide.

Sarain opened the blacked-out glass door, and stepped into the small lobby of the club where a large bouncer stood with another smaller man at a register, while loud music thumped, vibrating the room. Behind them were dark heavy curtains, which Sarain could only assume were there to hide the view of the dancers that might be on stage, from people who had just walked in off the street. The man behind the register gave Sarain a long look before asking, "Are you here to apply or are you here to look?" Sarain didn't know how to answer at first, before she finally settled on muttering, "I'm here to look." "Nice," the man replied with a sly smile, and then stated, "You get in free, honey. Someone like you can only help our business." The man then stamped her hand, while the bouncer pulled back the curtain to let her inside.

Flashing strobe lights and colorful spotlights lit the room, and poorly at that. The seats and tables that the customers sat at were mostly dark, making it hard for Sarain to see what anyone looked like and if Winston was there. Only the runway and the bar had lights to clearly see.

So as not to attract attention to her, Sarain sat down at an empty table in the back, and tried her best to scan the crowd for Winston. Without her old demonic ability to see in the dark, Sarain found it nearly impossible to make out the faces of all the patrons. Sarain decided to wait there for a while, hoping to get a better look at a couple of questionable men. Sarain turned her gaze away as the dancers came on stage; she had no need or interest in seeing the girls work, and only cared to see what the men who surrounded them looked like. The men hollered and whistled each time the dancers removed an article of clothing, with all eyes on them, except for Sarain's, and one man's.

While Sarain adverted her eyes from the entertainment, she noticed that one man also wasn't watching the women dance, but instead was fixated on her. His eyes weren't glowing, but still his stare bothered Sarain, causing her to wonder if the patron was more than a man. His stare was constant and intensive, and Sarain could at least see that this man was not Winston.

After a few minutes of awkward staring, the man got up and walked over to Sarain's table, where he sat down and then asked, "Can I buy you a drink?" "No...thank you," Sarain replied, while still trying to see the other men's faces. "Do you come here often?" the man asked. "No," she simply responded. "You're very beautiful, much more than the girls on the stage; you put them to shame," he said trying to be charming. Sarain gazed at the man, and realized that he was no demon, but just a regular guy trying to hit on her. She gave a quick glance to the other men in the room and then sighed; she didn't feel as though Winston was among those men, though was perhaps half hoping.

Sarain stood up, and turned toward the exit. "Hey!" the man called out as she walked away, but made no effort to follow her. Sarain left the club with the two men up front also watching her closely. She stepped out into the musky night air, not knowing where next to look for Winston. She sighed again, wondering if he could be waiting back at home, and she began to walk in the direction of Wormwood Alley. She had only taken a few steps when the sound of moaning came from the alleyway near her. Sarain immediately remembered the prostitutes she had seen earlier walking the street, and became disgusted at the thought that one might be working only a few feet away from her. Still, Sarain couldn't help but let her eyes gaze down the alley where she saw a man and a woman standing, The woman's back was toward Sarain, and all she could see of the man was a tuff of hair as he leaned over, kissing the woman's neck.

Sarain began to walk on, when a smell suddenly caused her to stop. It was a familiar smell, one that sadly Sarain had become very used to during her years of hunting; it was the smell of blood. She glanced back down the alley again, this time trying to get a better look at the couple, and that's when she saw the line of blood trickling down the back of the woman's neck, and realized that the man was not kissing her at all.

"Hey!" Sarain instinctively called out, before remembering that she was unarmed, and the man's head quickly jerked up. It was then that Sarain gasped, as she looked into the vil sang's glowing eyes. He let the woman's limp body drop to the ground, when he recognized the teary interrupter.

Tears rolled down Sarain's cheeks as she turned away and ran. The vil sang immediately chased after her, grabbing at her arm. Sarain screamed, tugging her arm away, and then cried out, "Get away from me, Winston!" "Wait, you don't understand!" Winston frantically tried to explain, "This isn't about sex! She's just someone that no one will miss!" "What!?" the confused Sarain replied with shock. "The streets are better without people like her!" Winston responded.

Sarain began to think about Shaven's lack of criminal activity lately, and suddenly became very pale. After a few seconds of silence, her body quivered, and she immediately bent over and began to vomit. Tears welled in Winston's eyes as he watched the sickness that Sarain was feeling, and he knew that he was going to lose her. He tried to help her up from her position on the ground once she stopped puking, but Sarain quickly swatted Winston away.

"Leave me alone!" she shouted at him, and she began to run once again. "Sarain!" he called out chasing after her, but then stopped as she turned the corner. Winston stood there, not to let Sarain go, but because something else suddenly took precedence over trying to stop Sarain and it was the sensation that was growing in his body. Pain shot up into Winston's head, and down his spine. He felt his eyes burn inside his head, his muscles tightened, and his skin seared.

Winston fell to his knees as his body began to convulse, and he knew that what Alorea had said earlier that night was true; his body was changing.

Chapter 19

Sarain raced through the chilly night breeze, gasping and crying, as she thought of what she had just seen. She couldn't believe that Winston was killing and feeding on people even if they were criminals. Winston had claimed to have been feeding on animals the past year, and maybe he was, but not the kind of animals he had led Sarain to believe. Before she had died, Sarain had always known Winston to feed on willing partners, and never to kill them. He had claimed that doing so left him with a constant supply of blood, and no bodies to lead hunters to his door, but now something had changed. Sarain could possibly fathom Winston killing while he was grieving after her death, but now that she had returned, she couldn't understand why he would continue hunting people.

Something about Winston had changed, and Sarain found herself becoming scared of him. She couldn't go home, because it was his home, so she ran to the only place she felt safe: the chapel. David had told her that its doors would always be open for her, and tonight she hoped to find that true.

Sarain sprinted the whole way, with the wind drying her tears. She stopped for nothing, and even raced through busy streets, dodging cars and not stopping to catch her breath. As she approached the darkened church, she saw no lights on in its windows, and she prayed that the doors would be unlocked, for her, just as David had once said. Sarain took the stone steps slower than usual, as she exhaled heavily, her chest hurting from her speedy jog. Her hand went out to the angel statue as she passed it, to steady herself. She then reached for the handle of one of the doors, and with both hands, strained to pull it open. Her whole body sighed when the door groaned open; it was indeed unlocked, even at this late hour.

As Sarain shakily stepped inside, she immediately saw David at the altar, relighting the candles that were the only source of light in the room. He quickly lifted his head, with a look of surprise upon his face to see her stepping through the door. "Are you okay?" he asked, moving towards Sarain as she approached. Sarain didn't reply, but instead continued to stagger, breathlessly, toward David, and as she neared him her knees began to buckle. David's arms abruptly shot out as he dove forward, allowing Sarain to crash into his embrace. Sarain panted with exhaustion, trying to catch her breath before stammering out, "He, he's feeding on people." "Oh, Sarain, I'm sorry," David replied. Sarain began to cry again, as she clung to the priest, and mumbled, "I think he's been killing Shaven's criminals." David sighed, and then remarked, "That would explain the dramatic drop of crime here, lately… But even if his victims are criminals, it doesn't make what he's doing okay." "I know that… It's why I'm here," Sarain stated, still holding on to David as she said, "I'm afraid that I can't trust him; I don't know him anymore."

David stroked Sarain's hair to calm her, and once her breathing had returned to normal, she began to pull away from him. She stood up straight, letting go of David, and took a step back. "I'm sorry about my composure," Sarain muttered, with tears still on her face. "Don't worry, I'm glad you came to me," he kindly stated. Then while looking down at her, he reached up and wiped away the trail of Sarain's tears off her cheek, and for a moment, his hand lingered against her skin. Sarain stared up at David, staying very still, as his eyes locked with hers. In that instant, it felt as though one of them should have made a move toward the other, but neither did. Instead, David moved his hand away from her as Sarain took another step back. Both their gazes went to the ground, and Sarain broke the awkward silence by asking, "Is there anywhere that I can stay for the night?" The question didn't help the awkwardness, as it made David blush, but after a second to compose himself, he replied, "We have a guest room, in case of emergencies, like this." "Good," Sarain quickly said, and then corrected, "I mean thanks."

David led Sarain out of the chapel, and into a connecting building. In this building were all the normal things you would expect to see in a home; a kitchen, a bathroom, a den with many bookcases filled with books, and there were pictures of priests and staff that had served at the church over the years. David continued walking past these things and down a long hallway, where he turned to Sarain and held a finger up to his lips to let her know to be quiet here. He led her down that hall to one of the doors at the end. David opened the door and switched on a light, and Sarain saw a simple room with a twin sized bed, a lamp, and a small dresser. A cross hung on the wall above the bed, but other than that there were no decorations in the plain white-walled room.

"I hope this meets your standards," David said in a hushed tone. "It's perfect," Sarain whispered back. He smiled, and then stated, "My room is two doors down, on the left, if you need anything. There are extra blankets in the bottom drawer of the dresser, if you get cold... Sleep well." "You too," Sarain replied, and then watched as David left, walking down the hall, and to his room. He gave her one last glance before entering his room and closing the door behind him, and she then did the same.

Sarain sat down on the bed, and gazed up at the cross that hung up on the wall. She stared for a long while, as though she was looking for some sort of answer in the religious object, but all she found was a symbol that felt empty to her. It was then that Sarain felt the tears begin to run down her cheeks again, and with a sudden surge of emotion, she quickly grabbed the pillow on the bed and buried her face into it. She muffled her cries, as she screamed into the pillow, practically inhaling the fabric, but she did not want to wake any of the sleeping worshippers.

When Sarain finally felt calm enough to pull the pillow away, she felt a shiver go down her spine, but she knew no amount of extra blankets would help with this chill. Only Winston knew how to soothe Sarain, but after what she had seen that night, she felt as though she would never feel the same again. Her hopes and peace had been shattered, and now all she could feel was loss and regret.

And for a moment, she wished she had never returned from the dead.

It was a clear blue day, with the sun shining high up in the sky, and the trees were at their greenest. Sarain swung back and forth, dragging her feet in the sand with each glide backwards. She sat on the swing in her best dress; it was red with polka dots and white lace along the edges. Her hair was pulled into pigtails just as her mother always liked to do it, and she held onto the rope of the handmade swing, tightly, as a pair of strong hands gently pushed her forward. Sarain's pigtails swayed with each push, and it gave the sides of her head a funny feeling that made the young Sarain feel like giggling even though the swinging itself scared her a little.

"Are you having fun?" a male voice asked from behind her, "Do you want to go higher?" "I don't want to go faster, it's too scary," she spoke in a soft voice. "Don't worry, nothing bad will happen to you with me here," he replied. "But something bad has already happened," she muttered with a faint memory in the back of her mind. "Shh, forget about that; it's as though it never happened. Here it's just you and me, as it should have been," he whispered.

Sarain swung back and forth a few more times, now feeling a little fuzzy and confused, sensing that something wasn't right. Finally she said softly, "No, this isn't right; you were never here." Sarain immediately found herself sitting fully grown on the motionless swing. It was quiet for a moment, making her begin to wonder if he still stood there behind her. "No...I wasn't, but I wish I had been...I wish I could have been the father that you needed," he finally replied, sadly, "I would have given anything to hear you call me 'Dad'."

Sarain's grip tightened even more around the rope; she had wondered if he would ever visit her, like the others, or if he even could. Sarain took a deep breath, and finally mustered the strength to turn around and gaze upon her visitor. The beautiful day ceased to exist behind her, instead there was an empty blackness, and in that nothingness stood one thing, Aion. He lacked the same grand and fearful luster that he had had in life, now instead he stood, a mere man, as he had once been a millennia ago.

"Why are you here?" Sarain asked. "To ask for your forgiveness," Aion replied. "...I'm sorry, but I can't give you that... I can understand your hatred for my clan, and I can even understand why you used Orran as you did, but I could never forgive you for killing Eddie," she said with all honesty. Aion nodded in agreement, as though he had already anticipated her answer; "I figured as much, but I had to come and see you anyway... There is something else I need your forgiveness for." Sarain stared upon him with curiosity as Aion enlightened, "That last night, I didn't wait for you the whole time on that mountain top...As soon as I sensed that you were alone, I paid a visit to your companion." Sarain's eyes widened as Aion continued, "I couldn't take the chance that you would win, and so I left you a parting gift just in case... I fed him my blood." Sarain sighed, "Oh

Winston," she muttered, now understanding why he seemed so different. "How do I stop it?" she asked her father. "I don't know if you can," Aion answered.

Sarain shuttered, and a strong breeze immediately blew between the two. What surroundings that had existed began to fade into blackness until only they remained. "I am so sorry, my child," Aion said, with him too beginning to fade. His figure was slowly becoming transparent, and he gazed upon her with a sad smile as he stated, "I won't be able to visit you again, and all I can do for you is hope that you can somehow find happiness."

Aion's image became a faint blur, and knowing that his time was nearly up, he quickly said, "Before I died that day, in your arms, my last thought...my last wish was for you to not come with me...I'd give my very soul for you to know a better life." And with that, Aion was gone, leaving Sarain alone.

She woke up soon after with the sun barely rising outside. Sarain thought of how she had returned to life, as a mortal, and she wondered if that was what Aion had wished for, and why he would not be able to visit her in a dream again. Had he used his own soul so that she could have a second chance at life?

Chapter 20

Sarain lay there in bed staring up at the hints of light that were barely starting to illuminate the room. Flecks of light shined in through the blinds on the window, and Sarain assumed that the church's staff would soon be getting up. She thought of Winston, and how heartbroken he had seemed when she had run from him the night before. She hadn't understood then why his actions had led him to such an act, but now after what the vision of Aion had told her, she realized why Winston had seemed to be not only regressing in their relationship, but why he was becoming more aggressive; Aion's demonic blood was eating away at his humanity.

Sarain thought of the demonic vil sang siblings, Cyrus and Desmina that she had fought against years ago; they had been results of Aion's blood. She thought of Sephor, who had once been Aion's general, he had completely forgotten his human life, and Kayne, whose bat-like wings made him look like a gargoyle from gothic artwork. Aion's blood always seemed to have the result of making a vil sang turn more demonic like that of a full-fledged demon. The only exception was Orran, who never fully turned into a vil sang; he had the strength, the speed, and the fast healing, but had none of the weaknesses or the need to feed on blood.

Sarain wasn't sure what Aion's blood would do to Winston, but from what it had done so far, the end result couldn't be good. She thought about everything they had been through: the battles, the longing, the lust, the love, and the regret. She felt as though she had failed Winston in the past, and she didn't want to make that mistake again.

In that moment, Sarain decided that she would return to Winston; she couldn't abandon him again, not when he needed her the most. She just prayed that there was something she could do to help him, to stop what was happening to him.

Sarain rose out of bed quietly and quickly, she didn't want to disturb those who were still sleeping, and she especially didn't want to alert David of her actions; if he knew that she was planning to go back to Winston he would surely try to stop her. Sarain swiftly snuck out of the church by slipping out her window. She knew David would worry about her, and she had thought about leaving him a note, but then she realized that there was nothing she could say that could rationalize what she was doing, because what she was feeling in her heart wasn't rational.

The walk back to Winston's house seemed long as Sarain contemplated what she might say to him. She thought of what she could truly do to help him, and other than being open and honest with him, there was nothing she could do than simply be there for him as Aion's blood worked its course through Winston's body.

Sarain wondered how Winston would be when she got home; would he be distraught? Would he be glad to see her or would he be angry? It seemed like both their first instincts were to fight, even when it came to each other. Sarain had wished that this was a result of demon blood, but she knew this wasn't true since she no longer carried it inside of her. Sarain never knew much more than fighting, so it wasn't a surprise that she always went to it first, but now that her body wasn't equipped to be the warrior she once was, she had to find a new way to handle things.

The sun was getting brighter with the dawn at full force. The morning dew was quickly drying up from the desert landscape that was Wormwood Alley. Sarain stopped in her tracks and stared off in front of her once Winston's house came in view.

It was now or never, Sarain thought to herself. She couldn't run away from this problem, Winston needed her. Life had been so much simpler when she was a hunter; fight or flight, and keep everything else at a distance, because attachments only led to pain. The theory still held true even now; her attachment to Winston was causing her pain, and she had to either stay and fight for him, or leave and start a new life. Nothing about her life with Winston had ever been simple, but it was with him that she had experienced some of the best moments in her life too. He was the one that had given her faith in people again; had it not been for him saving her over and over again, she would be lost if not dead, and he was the only reason worth coming back from the grave.

Sarain took a deep breath, and then finished her walk to the house. She stood in front of the door for a moment, preparing herself for however she might find Winston inside, before finally opening the door.

Sarain walked in to see Winston sitting on the couch as if he had been waiting for her all along. He looked tired as though he hadn't slept, and the house was in disarray. The kitchen table and chairs had been smashed to pieces, but this wasn't what concerned Sarain, what really caught her attention was that her backpack appeared to be packed and sitting at Winston's feet.

"What is that doing there?" Sarain asked referring to her bag. "I figured I'd make it easier on the both of us," he muttered. "I wasn't planning on leaving," she remarked, with Winston quickly replying, "Well you could have fooled me with how disgusted you were with me last night, and then not coming home until morning… You were with him, weren't you?" "Really? That's what you think we should talk about, and not what I witnessed last night?" Sarain stated with annoyance. "I can smell him on you!" Winston said angrily. "Nothing happened, Winston! And nothing will ever happen, because I'm in love with you!" she yelled. "Well you shouldn't be!" he shouted back, "I'm not good for you." Sarain began to approach Winston as she said, "That's not true…" But he cut her off by quickly saying, "I've been killing people, Sarain!" "You've been killing criminals, and even that's not really your fault; I know what Aion did to you," she immediately replied. "That's impossible," he commented, and then she muttered, "I know he fed you his blood." "And? So what, I've had demon blood in me for decades. I'm the one who killed those people, not your father!"

Winston shouted. "I've seen what happens to people who carry his blood, and they become monsters," Sarain remarked. "You didn't," he quickly said. "Not fully… But I was starting to, or have you forgotten about the claws I grew, and the other changes I went through before I died?" she replied.

Winston sighed, and Sarain continued to move towards him, until finally she sat down next to him on the couch. She placed her hand on top of his, and gently whispered, "I'm not going to let you go through this alone." They sat in silence for a while after that with Sarain continuing to hold Winston's hand. She was waiting for him to say something since she didn't know what to say herself.

A tear ran down Winston's cheek as he took a deep breath before finally saying, "You should go." Sarain looked up at him with surprise, as he said, "You shouldn't be with me, Sarain, especially for this." "But," she started to say when he cut her off, "No, this isn't like one of our battles, we're not going to beat this, and I don't want you wasting your life watching me turn into a monster." "Winston, I can't just leave you," she pleaded. "Come on," he spoke more forcefully, "You have before, and now I truly am a monster." She began to cry as she said, "No you're not, you're the man I love." "Damn it, Sarain! Why couldn't you have been this way a year ago?" Winston shouted, "You just had to continue chasing after Aion when we could have been together!" She stared at him stunned as he continued to yell, "I didn't care that you had claws or pointed ears, and so what if you were turning into a vil sang, I could have shown you how to live my life." "But that's not what I wanted," she stated with frustration. "We could have been together forever!" he declared. "Yeah, but as demons!" she cried. "That's what I am, Sarain! And that's all I'll ever be!" Winston screamed at her. "But I can't be!...That life, and the life I was leading before that as a hunter, I couldn't do it anymore," Sarain explained, "I was so sick of not being a part of the life that I was allowing everyone else to have, and the thought of spending an eternity killing other demons while I lived as one was too much for me to bare!" "What are you saying?" he questioned. "I'm saying, that I chose to die instead," she revealed.

Winston's eyes went wide, and after a moment to take in what he had just heard, his expression changed from shock to rage. "You're saying that you chose to kill yourself rather than live with me, like me?" he spoke with a deep and billowing anger building up. "…..Yes," Sarain simply replied. He looked amazed, and continued to glare at her as he stated, "Your death put me through hell! I lost myself, Sarain! You dying changed me more than your father's blood ever did!" "I'm sorry, but I had to put a stop to everything. Winston it wasn't about you, if the choice had truly just been about living as a vil sang with you, than I likely would have thought differently, but that wasn't the case, that choice meant leaving Aion alive. And I couldn't let him continue with his plans to dominate mankind," she tried to explain. "So you chose your mission over me then," Winston stated matter-of-factly. "Winston," she said with a sigh, "I had to." He rolled his eyes, and she then added, "But it was still an error that I'll never make again." "No," he spoke, turning towards her, "You made your choice. You wanted a life without demons and fighting, well you're human now, and you can have that." Sarain then reached out to embrace Winston, saying, "But I don't want a life without you."

Winston quickly moved away from her, and said, "But you deserve better… There's nothing I can give you or do for you now, but just cause you pain… I don't want you wasting your second chance of life to fulfill some sort of loyalty to me." "But it's my choice," she said. "No," he quickly replied, "It's my choice too." He then picked up her bag, and tried to hand it to her, but she wouldn't take it.

"Take it," he ordered firmly, but she simply answered, "No." Winston then grabbed Sarain by the arm and pulled her to the door where he opened it and threw her bag outside. Not caring for his own wellbeing, he pushed her out the door with such force that he allowed his hands and arms to be scorched by the sun that was now brightly shining outside.

"Winston!" Sarain cried out as he slammed and locked the door behind him. She pounded her fists against the door, hoping that Winston would change his mind, and let her back in, but the door never opened. She collapsed to her knees and began to cry, not knowing what she would do next, or for the rest of her life… without Winston.

Chapter 21

With the sun still shining high up in the sky, Sarain felt she had no other choice, but to wander the desolate outskirts of Shaven. She didn't want to face David at the moment, knowing that he would be worried and likely upset with her for leaving without a word. She didn't feel up for any more drama, and wanted time alone to find clarity, so she walked the desert landscape of Wormwood Alley. She trekked until she reached the mountain range; this made her think of when she and Orran escaped from the Brotherhood's cavernous headquarters, with the two of them so desperately racing to get out into the sunlight and away from Kayne and her father's other demonic minions.

And for a second a thought flashed into her mind of how she had ruined the lives of all the men who had come into hers. The thought immediately made Sarain's stomach turn, and she quickly forced it out of her mind by trying to focus on the scenery around her. She walked around the rocky base of the mountainside until she reached a wooded region. It was a remarkable change of landscape, going from desert to forest in literally just a few steps. The woods were dense and very green; fallen branches and trees were scattered about with lots of moss and grass covering them and the ground; Sarain had to carefully watch her every step. Even without use of a map, Sarain felt as though she knew exactly where she was headed, but it wasn't confirmed until a familiar structure came into view. The house looked a little more overgrown with plant life than she recalled, but otherwise it was virtually untouched; Orran's safe house was just as she remembered it.

The grass and shrubbery had become tall and thick; it reached Sarain's waist as she made her way towards the house, and when she neared the front of the house, she noticed an object hidden by the grass that she hadn't seen before. As Sarain approached the object she soon realized what it was. With a large mound of dirt at its base, the structure stood straight up out of the ground; it was a crudely made wooden cross, and carved into it was Orran's name. She was standing at her friend's grave, knowing that there was only one way that his remains could have been laid to rest there…Winston. He must have gone back to that mountainside to retrieve Orran's body, and then carried him all the way to this old house to bury him.

Sarain dropped to her knees, no longer able to force her feelings away; she began to weep for her departed friend. She had gotten Orran back after believing him dead for so many years only to lose him again so quickly, and he had died trying to protect her. She thought of how Winston must have felt compelled to bury her friend, despite the fact that they had both competed for her heart. They had at one point hated each other, but in the end, they had seemed to grow a respect for one another; whether it was only for Sarain's benefit, she wasn't sure, but Orran had once saved Winston's life, and so perhaps that was why Winston had felt obligated to give him a proper burial.

Sarain recalled when the three of them trained for the fight against the Brotherhood; with high hopes in their hearts everything seemed both monumental and simpler back then somehow. Sarain recalled how Orran had initially wanted to run, but she was the one who opted to fight with Winston blindly following her every command. She realized that it was her decision that had gotten her and Orran killed and now left Winston doomed for damnation. She thought about what Winston had said to her, about how they should have run away together, and knew that if she had listened to her friends they would likely all be alive now. Whether stopping Aion had been the right decision or not didn't seem to matter anymore; now, Sarain just missed her loved ones, and wanted things to go back to the way they were.

Her life had become a mess, and the mere thought of it turned her stomach. In fact, it turned her stomach so much so that she suddenly found herself stumbling away from Orran's grave so that she could cough up the vomit that had risen in her throat, away from her friend's final resting place. Sarain gagged and heaved until nothing but air came out, and then she struggled to catch her breath. Tears flooded from her eyes as she kneeled with her hands against the ground.

She heard the voice inside her head begging to be told what to do. What could she do now that she was alone and unable to fight? What of life was there left for her to live? She wanted an answer or a savior; something, anything to tell her what to do next.

Winston sat there on the couch, slouching back as he emptied another bottle of tequila. It was hard for a vil sang to get drunk, but after his third bottle of the best brand of tequila that Shaven had to offer, Winston was finally starting to feel its effects. He threw the empty bottle down, and quickly grabbed another out of the hefty triple-bagged supply he had gotten that night from Shaven's liquor store.

Winston didn't want to feel anything that night; he didn't want to feel anything for a long while. He had ended things with Sarain, and that was something he thought he'd never do; she had been his whole world and every dream over the past decade, and the idea that he would ever be the one to toss her aside didn't fathom as real. But the truth was that Winston would rather let Sarain go then subject her to the changes he was going through; he knew that likely the worst was yet to come, and he loved Sarain too much to put her through the madness of seeing him become a true demon.

Winston was halfway through his fourth tequila bottle when a knock came upon his door. His first thought was that Sarain had come back, and in his liquor fueled stupor he staggered up to answer the door, knowing full well that he had to shut Sarain out of his life completely if he was going to spare her the agony of seeing him transform into a monster, but at the same time, Winston wanted more than anything to see Sarain on the other side of that door.

He swayed drunkenly as he swung open the door, only to have his hopes quickly dashed when he saw Alorea standing on the other side. "What are you doing here?" he immediately snarled with disappointment in his voice. "What a greeting," Alorea chimed, "You're even more somber than usual; what's got your panties in a bunch?" Alorea pushed past Winston to quickly get into his house before he could close the door on her. Her eyes immediately took in the sight of his trashed home, and she turned to him and remarked, "What happened here? Did you have a fight with your female?" "That's none of your business," Winston abruptly shot back. A grin began to form on Alorea's face as she said, "You did fight, didn't you? Could it be that she has finally decided to leave you, again?" Winston didn't answer, but instead walked back to the couch and flopped down on it. He picked up his bottle of tequila and resumed drinking.

Alorea stared down at Winston, and with a grunt said, "Well that's rude of you to not offer your guest something to drink, but, anyway, the reason I am here is to see if you have given any thought to the Brotherhood's offer?" "What are you, their secretary now?" Winston muttered in between swigs of tequila. "They thought it best if I was their liaison, yes, but it's not the only reason I am here," Alorea answered. "Well, tell them that they can shove their offer, and as for whatever you're offering…Well, you know where the door is, see yourself to it," Winston replied crudely.

Alorea frowned, and then stated, "I think you're making a mistake…On both offers. Winston, you have a chance here to really have something; the Brotherhood wants you to lead them into a new era; to be a leader like no other. And with me at your side you'll want for nothing, you can become more powerful than you have ever been, and have an army at your disposal." "I don't want an army," he muttered. "No, you want an unrealistic life with a woman that neither wants nor needs you! Do you think that that human will stay by your side if you continue to change with the power growing inside you? Can she hunt with you? Can she even stand to see you feed?" Alorea dramatically questioned him, and then added, "I am willing, and wanting to be with you, Winston! I love you with every inch of my being, and will do anything to show you!"

Alorea suddenly moved towards Winston, who still lay on the couch. She quickly climbed up and straddled him before he even removed the bottle from his lips. He gazed up at her with his eyes looking somewhat glazed over, he finally moved his bottle of tequila away from his mouth, and he shifted his torso upward from underneath Alorea, but he didn't push her away. "You really still love me after all this time, and after the way I've treated you?" Winston asked with curiosity. "Of course I do," Alorea practically moaned with excitement. She leaned down, pressing her body against his, and moved her lips towards Winston's, but at the last second he turned his face away from hers. Alorea hesitated for only a moment from Winston's subtle refusal to kiss her. She instead began kissing his cheek, to his jaw, and then down his neck. Her hands moved up underneath Winston's shirt, and she ran her fingers against his abs and to his chest. Alorea rubbed up against him, hoping to make him as aroused as she was, but Winston continued to simply lie there neither stopping her nor participating. She caressed her hand up from underneath his shirt, and began to lift off Winston's top, and still he didn't stop her.

Alorea threw Winston's shirt to the ground, and she started kissing his chest. As she dragged her tongue gently against the curves of Winston's abs, she felt him begin to shift beneath her. Winston's hands went to Alorea's waist, and for a moment, she thought that he was going to throw her off, but then she felt him suddenly pull her up closer towards him. Winston's hand went to Alorea's cheek, and he pulled her in for a kiss. Alorea hungrily pressed her lips against his, and then parted them so that she could slip her tongue into his mouth. She closed her eyes, and moaned when his tongue stroked against hers. When she felt Winston's hands moving to pull off her blouse, she softly muttered, "See, I can make you happy, just as I did the last time that woman left you."

Winston's hands suddenly stopped, and Alorea opened her eyes to see him staring up at her sternly. He said with a firm tone, "You never made me happy, you were just convenient." "But I'm the one who's here with you!" Alorea whined hoping to make Winston see things her way. "Only because I threw Sarain out," Winston remarked. "You threw her out? Why would you do that if you're so in love with her?" Alorea asked confused. "Because she's better off with that priest," he grumbled. Alorea's eyes went wide, "There's a priest involved with Sarain? Are they romantic?" "Why does that matter? Like you really care what she does with another guy," he stated. "Damn it, Winston, how can you be so stupid? The churches around here are filled with a bunch of religious hunters! If this priest knows about you, then no wonder he's come between you and Sarain, he's probably using her to get information on you. Come on, if the Brotherhood can sense your growing power, surely others can too," Alorea enlightened with panic in her voice. "You really think he's using Sarain?" Winston hazily muttered half to himself and half out loud. "You should probably be more concerned with the question of whether or not Sarain is flat out working with this guy. She is a hunter after all, and if she was able to hunt down and kill her own father, then I see no problem with her doing the same to you. Besides, she hasn't been all that loyal to you in the past; after all, that's how we got together in the first place," Alorea proclaimed.

"I can't believe that she would use me, though," Winston commented. "Whether she is or isn't, you know she's keeping something from you, something that likely involves that priest; why else would she be mixed up with him when she has you?" Alorea questioned. Winston tried to contemplate the theory over, through his drunken haze; Sarain had insisted that David was just a friend, and led him to believe that he was helping her with her new found humanity, but for a while now, Winston had felt as though Sarain was hiding something from him.

"You need to put a stop to this priest; he knows too much about you," Alorea advised, "And if Sarain is spending so much time with this man, then she can't be trusted either." Winston's gaze settled on Alorea as he solemnly asked, "What do you suggest I do?" "You need to find out where her loyalties lie; you need to kill the priest," Alorea replied.

Chapter 22

The flame flickered as he tried to light the wick of the candle, and once its waxy stem took ablaze, he moved the long matchstick to the next white candle. David lit each candle with a prayer, as he did every night before he locked up the church. The chapel stood dark and empty; all parishioners had long since left, and as the youngest staff member and priest, the job of locking up was his responsibility.

All was quiet, with only the sounds of David's footsteps echoing through the hall as he made his way to the chapel doors. It was very late; David had been stalling as long as he could before he finally decided to lock the chapel doors. He had hoped that Sarain would show up; his thoughts had been clouded with worry for her since he found the guest room empty that morning.

As David approached the chapel's double doors, he noticed that one of the doors was ever so slightly ajar. This seemed somewhat odd, since most of the parishioners knew to pull the doors until they loudly groaned shut with a click, but it wasn't entirely strange since David could not recall if he ever heard or checked to see if the doors had been properly closed earlier. He shrugged it off, but then decided to pull the door open fully so that he could check to make sure that nothing had obstructed the door, such as litter or debris.

David glanced around the entryway, but there was nothing on the ground or around the door's frame that could have jammed it. So he began to close the heavy door when he noticed a feminine figure standing on the chapel's steps, and his first thought was of Sarain, and the hope that she had returned. But it took only a moment for him to see the blond hair and pale skin that didn't belong to his friend. David's composure immediately shifted as he tensed up, and said with his deepest, strongest tone, "Your kind is not welcomed here."

Alorea gazed up at David, from her position on the steps, looking slightly ill, as she asked, "Is it that easy for you to recognize what I am?" "It is when you get that sick just being near a cross," he observed, and then firmly stated, "You need to leave this place." "I'm not leaving until you answer some questions first," Alorea declared while staring up at the young priest. "I have nothing to say to a devil whore like you," David announced, and then backed up into the church. He was about to close the chapel door when a hand shot out from behind him and grabbed the door, stopping it from closing. Before David could turn around to see who had interfered, he felt himself being shoved violently through the doorway. The young priest fell to the ground, in front of the smirking Alorea. He immediately gazed up, with his vision slightly blurred to observe the somewhat familiar face of someone he wasn't pleased to see: Winston.

"You," David abruptly blurted out, "I knew Sarain couldn't trust you." "Can't trust me? Really? What lies have you been feeding her?" Winston angrily questioned. "I have no use for lies," David quickly said in his defense, "Sarain comes to me because she doubts your loyalty," he then glanced at Alorea, and remarked, "And it looks like she was right too." "Bullshit, Sarain knows she's everything to me; no other woman could ever compare to her," Winston replied without delay, not seeing the hurt it put in Alorea's eyes. "You had to have done or said something to her to put those doubts there!" "I would never betray her trust like that!" David declared.

Winston moved toward David, and pulled him up from the ground. He stared down into the gray eyes of the vulnerable, but brave young man, and said, "I'm not an idiot; I can tell that you're in love with her," Winston drew David closer to him as he stated, "I just want to know what it is that keeps her coming here to see you." A look of realization suddenly came over David's face, and he said, almost with a smile, "She never told you." Winston forcefully shook him as he yelled, "Told me what!" He threw David back to the ground and shouted, "Did you fuck her?!"

"No," a voice said from the base of the stone steps. Winston's gaze immediately went to where the voice had originated, and he saw Sarain standing there, her backpack flung over one shoulder, and her staring up at him with rage in her eyes. "Leave him alone," she demanded. Winston took a step away from David, while continuing to stare intensely down at Sarain, and then he began to take a step down the stone stairs, towards her.

"No, you don't get to come near me!" Sarain shouted, "You can't throw me out, and then act like you're the one who's hurt!" "But I made a mistake, Sarain; I love you too much to let you go!" Winston responded in an outburst. "No," she quickly shot back, seeing him take another step towards her, "If you really loved me you wouldn't be harassing the only friend that I have! And you wouldn't be here with her!" "He's trying to take you away from me," Winston said as though attempting to explain his actions. "The only person here who's trying to break us up is that slut over there," Sarain replied looking towards Alorea.

"Don't listen to her! The priest already admitted that she's keeping stuff from you! Winston, she's not invested in your relationship; she was obviously coming here to be with him," Alorea shouted, trying to persuade him. Winston's gaze shifted from Alorea, and then back to Sarain as he asked, "Why are you here?" "Like I said, David is my only friend; you threw me out, where else am I going to go?" Sarain answered with annoyance. "Come back home with me then, and we can straighten this whole mess out together," Winston stated as he stretched his hand out towards her. Sarain stared up at him for a moment, and then her eyes went past him and to David who remained on the ground where Winston had thrown him, leaving him sore and tussled. Alorea stood nearby, staring daggers at Sarain, and all this reminded her of how Winston had been when she first met him so many years ago.

"No," Sarain muttered shaking her head, "You were right before; we're only hurting each other being together. And whatever you're going through…..these changes, I can't help you...In fact; I think I'm making them worse." "You're just going to abandon him?" scoffed a surprised Alorea, "This is all your fault in the first place!" "Shut up!" Sarain shouted at her, "You're getting what you want; a chance to have him all to yourself!"

Winston looked wounded as he let his hand fall back to his side. "Have you stopped loving me then?" he asked sounding heartbroken. Sarain slightly shook her head, "No... I'll never stop loving you, but you're better off without me...I've ruined your life too many times." Winston sighed, and lowered his head as though he knew what Sarain was saying was true, and an awkward moment of silence past over all of them. Then suddenly, Winston's head shot back up with his piercing blue eyes a blazed, "No," he firmly stated, "I won't accept that; you are coming home with me!" He jumped down to the steps right in front of Sarain, and quickly grabbed a hold of her. She let out a yelp of surprise as she struggled with Winston's firm grasp on her. "Let her go!" she heard David call out from the top of the chapel's stone steps as he scurried to come to her aid.

Winston's arms wrapped tightly around Sarain as she shifted against him, trying to break free. Her face was pressed against his dense shoulder, but when she heard David cry out, Sarain managed to shift her head so that she could see why her friend had screamed. She saw Alorea with her arms wrapped around the young priest; she had snuck up behind him, and planted her fangs into the side of his neck.

"David!" Sarain screamed as she continued to try to break free from Winston's hold. She saw her friend quickly growing paler with each swallow of blood that Alorea took away from him. Winston's eyes glanced up to the grisly scene, but he neither did nor said nothing to stop Alorea. Sarain gazed up at Winston in disbelief, wondering if this had been his plan all along or if he just didn't care how he would get her all to himself.

Sarain watched as David slowly stopped struggling, and became limp in Alorea's arms. His eyes began to look lifeless until finally they rolled back into his head, and his knees buckled. David fell from Alorea's grasp with a heavy thud, causing Sarain to scream at the top of her lungs when she saw this. Her scream echoed out into the night as Alorea wiped the blood from her mouth, and said, "We better get going before people start showing up," looking towards Winston, and then she remarked, "Do you still want that traitor? Because if not, you better feed on her quick." Sarain looked up at Winston, also curious to the answer to Alorea's question, but she made no attempts to say anything to try and spare her life.

Winston looked down into Sarain's eyes expecting to see hate or disgust toward him, but instead all he saw was sorrow. Her eyes kept looking in David's direction, hoping that he would groan or move. Sarain didn't say anything to Winston, though he had hoped that she would, even if it was only to argue with him.

Finally Winston let his gaze move away from Sarain, and he loosened his grip on her. Sarain broke loose and immediately ran to David where she cradled his head and searched to find a pulse, with tears falling from her eyes.

Alorea watched the scene unfold with a look of shock upon her face as she reacted with irritation, "You're just going to let her go?" "Yes," Winston muttered, and then stated, "And you best keep your hands off her as well!" Alorea sighed in frustration, and began to leave down the stairs, and once she reached the bottom she looked back at Winston and asked, "Are you coming?"

Winston didn't answer, but instead gazed up at Sarain who only glanced at him for a moment before putting her attention back on to her fallen friend. Winston, without a word, proceeded to leave with Alorea.

Sarain kept her hands on David; cradling his head with her hands pressing against the wound on his neck as she watched, waiting for Winston and Alorea to be out of sight. When Sarain was sure that they were gone, she removed her hands from David's neck to see that the energy coming off her hands had already gotten the puncture wounds to scab over as though the injury had happened days ago. She looked down at David who was still very pale and barely breathing, "He lost too much blood," she thought to herself. Sarain moved her blood soaked hands towards David's chest, where she removed his collar, and unbuttoned his shirt. Sarain placed her hands over David's heart, against his now only lukewarm skin, and closed her eyes. She began to focus her thoughts, and envisioned in her mind, her hands inside David's chest and around his heart with the warmth from her hands gently helping his heart begin to beat stronger.

She pictured warm blood pumping through his veins and to all his limbs and organs. She took a deep breath as though the air she was inhaling would fill David's lungs, and then after a few seconds, opened her eyes and gazed upon him. The color had returned to David's skin, and as she stared down at him she noticed his eyelashes begin to flutter.

David opened his eyes to see Sarain watching over him with a smile upon her face and tears in her eyes. "Am I dead?" he muttered hoarsely, almost as faint as a whisper. "No," Sarain replied as a tear rolled down her cheek, "You're going to be just fine." "You healed me, didn't you?" he remarked with astonishment in his eyes, and Sarain answered him with a single nod. David shifted with a groan, and then his eyes moved down to where Sarain's hands still rested upon his chest. Sarain noticed the bashful look upon his face, and quickly moved her hands away from David.

After a minute went by for David to catch his bearings, Sarain helped him get back up on to his feet. She held on to his arm to keep him steady as she said, "You need to leave town quickly." David was taken aback by the comment, and when Sarain observed this, she explained, "It's best that Winston and Alorea believe that you're dead, otherwise they might come after you again." "That's a good point," he remarked, "I know a safe place I can go." "Good," Sarain replied, and then gazed at her friend and said in a soft tone, "Then I guess this is where we part ways."

Sarain abruptly moved in for a hug, knowing that David would be too shy to initiate one himself, and she gently wrapped her arms around him, hoping not to hurt his likely sore body. He seemed caught off guard by the action, but soon put his arms around her as well, and then to Sarain's surprise, she heard him say, "Come with me." She pulled away to see a very serious look upon David's face. She thought about her answer for a moment while David waited patiently for her response, and when she opened her mouth to reply, she was stopped by an unexpected feeling, a flutter from deep inside her. Her eyes went wide, and her breath caught in her throat.

David became alarmed by the sudden shift in Sarain's composure, and he anxiously asked her, "What's wrong?" She looked down with amazement as she placed a hand on her stomach in disbelief. "What is it?" David asked again, growing more concerned. Sarain smiled, and finally answered, "It's a miracle."

Chapter 23

Alorea paced the room as Winston sat in silence on the couch with his head in his hands; he hadn't spoken a word to her since they had gotten back to his house, and she was growing more and more impatient for him to make a move.

"The Brotherhood is going to want an answer soon," Alorea urged Winston, "They're getting tired of waiting, and if I don't tell them something soon, then they're going to approach you to press you for an answer one way or another." She glanced over at Winston to see that he hadn't moved from his position, so she blurted out, "Are you even listening to me? Do you have anything to say on the topic?" "I need to get her back," he muttered. Alorea stopped in her tracks and turned to Winston in annoyance, and said, "Are you serious? After everything she has put you through? Winston, she doesn't even want you! She went to that church to be with that priest!" "She said that she still loved me," he replied. "She probably just didn't want you to kill her," Alorea remarked. "No...I don't believe that," he muttered. "Don't be a fool, Winston, this isn't the first time she has abandoned you. She's an ignorant mortal, who only cares about herself. She'll age and die; she can't be there for you like I can, and she doesn't love you like I do," Alorea declared.

Winston suddenly lifted his head, and with a revelation, said, "You're right." Alorea smiled, and replied, "See, I knew you'd come around…Winston, you and I could do great things together…" But Winston suddenly cut her off by saying, "No, you were right about Sarain being a mortal. That's our problem; she's worried about me watching her die again! And that's where all our differences lie!" A look of anger came over Alorea's face as Winston proceeded on saying, "If she was a vil sang again, all our differences would go away. And with Aion gone, there's nothing to distract her or get in the way of our happiness!" "Are you crazy? You can't turn her!" Alorea declared. "She might resist at first, but I'm sure, afterwards, she'll see that it was the right decision," Winston stated as if talking to himself.

Alorea stormed over towards Winston, stood in front of him, and forced him to look up at her as she firmly said, "Winston, you can't turn Sarain; the Brotherhood won't allow it!" "What are you talking about; if they want me to lead them they'd have to expect that I'd want her by my side!" he commented. "She killed their last leader, they want nothing to do with her, mortal or not; they can't even stand knowing that she still lives," Alorea explained. "What are you saying?" Winston remarked, but already guessing what she was hinting at. "I'm saying that you should have killed her when you had the chance! It's going to be harder now, hunting her down with her on the run; she's made a life disappearing," Alorea replied.

Winston felt himself growing angry as he stared up at Alorea, and he said, "So you knew they wanted Sarain dead all this time?" "It should have been obvious, Winston," she replied, sarcastically. "Did they tell you to do it?" he asked curiously. "Only if you couldn't," Alorea answered, honestly, and then added, "They want me to be your queen... Winston, I will do this for you if you can't; I will kill her so that you can be free from the hold she has on you!" "You love me that much? Even though I love another woman?" he asked inquisitively. "Of course," Alorea said with excitement, "There's nothing you could do to make me stop loving you."

Winston stood up, and he gazed down into Alorea's blue eyes. She stared up at him lovingly, and the heaving of her breasts told him that she was becoming aroused with him staring and standing so near to her. Winston then brought his hand up to Alorea's cheek, and he brushed back a few strands of blond hair away from her face. He slid his hand gently down her neck and to her shoulder, and then he pulled her toward him. Winston leaned down and softly pressed his lips against Alorea's, and it only took a moment of kissing before she moaned and slipped her tongue into his mouth. Alorea groped at Winston hungrily, and as though following her unspoken request, Winston moved her toward the couch, and pushed her backward onto it. She pulled him down on top of her, and quickly began unbuttoning his shirt. Winston chuckled lightly, and whispered into Alorea's ear, "Slow down, there's no hurry. I want to do this right."

Alorea felt her body flutter in response to Winston's words, she felt happier than she had been in a long time. She smiled up at him as he began to lower his lips down to her neck, and he kissed it slowly. A passionate sigh escaped her mouth, and she began to arch her back with excitement when a sudden sharp and shocking pain went shooting through her throat. Alorea immediately grabbed onto Winston, and dug her nails into his back as she realized that he had just bitten her neck. Not sure at first if this was some kinky form of foreplay, Alorea didn't immediately fight back, but when she felt Winston's teeth clench down further, she knew that this wasn't a mere love bite. She immediately shrieked, and tried to push and kick Winston off of her, but his teeth dug down deeper. She felt his fangs break through her skin and burrow down into her flesh, and the agony of it throbbed throughout her body.

"Get off me!" Alorea strained to say, but Winston didn't comply, he instead began to pull her flesh away with his teeth. She tried to use her hands to hold the skin to her neck, to keep it together, but it was of no use, Winston jerked back his head taking a chunk of Alorea's throat with him. So much black blood gushed from Alorea's neck that she started to choke on it inside her own throat.

Alorea watched in horror as Winston swallowed the flesh that once belonged to her, with her dark blood dripping out his mouth. His eyes were ablaze as he scowled at her; then he let out a deep and animalistic growl. Before Alorea could run, Winston leapt on her like a lion on its prey, and he began further ripping at the wound he had started on her neck. Her screams came out as mere gurgles, and her attempts to fight were futile.

Alorea's vision was fading fast as darkness began to surround her, but as she took her last look at Winston, she saw him staring down at her with the cruelest of expressions, and the most violet pair of eyes.

Part 3

Chapter 24

Sarain found herself standing in a familiar looking room, but she couldn't quite place where she had seen it before. Everything had a strange hazy glow to it, as though the world around her wasn't real. "Am I dreaming?" Sarain asked herself.

Her eyes fell upon an object lying on the floor, in the center of the room. She took a few steps towards the item and soon saw that it was only a mere doll, but the doll itself seemed unusual, because it reminded her of one she had had as a child. In fact, this doll looked exactly like the one she had owned, scratches and all.

Sarain's gaze suddenly shot up to a door near her when she realized why the room had looked so familiar; it was one of the many places she had called home as a child, living amongst her nomadic clan. Sarain continued to stare at the door in front of her with amazement, and a little fear. She believed she knew what she would find on the other side, but wasn't sure she could handle it if her suspicions were true. A shiver went down Sarain's spine, and a tear escaped her eye before she finally took a deep breath, and stepped towards the door. The door was slightly ajar as she approached it, and it took only a small push to swing open. Inside Sarain saw not only what she recalled from many years ago, but she also saw things as though she had taken a step back from her own life; she saw herself, as a child, standing near her mother's bedside, trying hard to heal her sick and dying mom. Sarain watched as the two conversed, with her weak mother trying desperately hard to cheer up her young daughter.

Sarain gazed upon the memory, grateful to relive it, but not sure why she was there. Sarain sighed while staring down at her mother, and missing her greatly. Then suddenly, Ariana's eyes shifted from her young daughter to the Sarain that stood fully grown before her, and she looked her in the eye as she said, "You're going to have to be strong." Sarain felt her body tremble when she realized that her mother was staring at her, and then she found the courage to ask, "Why?" Her mother then replied, "He's going to need you." Sarain exhaled shakily, but her memory still recalled this conversation before, and she still wasn't sure if her mother was talking to the daughter who existed now and not the one who was truly with her during this moment, years ago.

Sarain watched as Ariana's eyes closed, and the young Sarain left her mother to rest, nearly walking through her grown, unseen self. The door gently closed behind Sarain, leaving her alone with her resting mother. She took a step closer to Ariana, whose breathing sounded shallow, and when she leaned in to check on her, she saw her mother's light brown eyes suddenly open; she wasn't asleep at all.

"I don't remember this," Sarain abruptly blurted out. "That's because it was a different you that was here last," Ariana replied. Sarain gasped, "You can see me?" "Of course, my sweet," her mother spoke again. "So then you were talking to me," Sarain remarked, and then asked curiously, "Who is it that needs me?" "The father of your child," Ariana stated. Sarain then looked down at her still flat stomach, and said, "You know that I'm pregnant?" "Of course I do, dear, I'm always with you," she replied. Sarain then looked back at her mother, and said, "But I've ruined Winston's life." Ariana gave her daughter a soft smile, and she stated, "His life didn't truly begin until he met you... And his soul can't be saved without you." "But I don't know how to save him," Sarain wept, "He's changed so much." "You'll know what to do when the time comes," Ariana simply replied, and then added, "But you need to hurry...Go to him...He needs you!"

Sarain felt herself being pulled to the door and away from her mother. She longed to stay by Ariana's side, but she knew that it was too late to save her mother. The door opened just as Sarain arrived to it, and she was quickly pulled back through it by an unseen force.

Sarain was immediately flooded with a light, and it took her several seconds before she recognized that she was lying in bed. She let out a sigh of relief, realizing that she was in no danger, and she nestled back into bed as she reflected on what she had just experienced. She wondered if she had merely been dreaming, or if she truly had visited her mom somehow. She knew that with everything that had happened in her life, anything was possible.

Sarain looked down at her stomach, and placed her hand against its warm skin. She began to think of Winston, as she had been doing every day for the past month since she last saw him, but this time she softly whispered with determination, "I'm going to get your daddy back, baby."

Sarain quickly dressed and went to find David somewhere on the grounds of the monastery; the same one he spoken of many times before they had arrived. They had been living there for the past month while she trained with monks, learning to hone her healing ability even better. When they had arrived at the monastery together, David had told the monks that Sarain was his sister, allowing them to remain together there, and in close quarters. He kept a watchful eye over her, and aided in caring for her prenatal needs, unsure of how the monks would take it if they discovered her pregnancy and the means by which she became that way. David had already been thinking of different possible cover stories they could tell the monks when Sarain's pregnancy came out. He particularly favored telling them that she had left an abusive relationship for the sake of her unborn child; he felt that wasn't too far from the truth, so that they wouldn't feel burdened by the sin of lying.

Sarain, on the other hand, hadn't really put much thought into what she would tell the monks. While she liked the serenity there and the capability to practice her healing ability openly, she always felt deep down that she wasn't going to be staying there long. She constantly found herself thinking of Winston, and longing to go back to Shaven to be with him, though it wasn't until that morning, after the vision of her mother, that she finally decided that it was time to go back. She worried about the safety of her child, Winston's likely worsening condition, and how David would take her leaving; but even with all these uncertainties Sarain couldn't turn her back on Winston if there really was a chance that she could save him. She may not know what exactly it was that she could do, but she suspected it lay with her healing ability. She just hoped that with all her training, she was now strong enough to stop Winston from getting any worse.

Sarain walked outside and into the weak but bright morning sun. She was immediately greeted by a cool gentle breeze as she walked the dirt path towards the monastery's garden, the place where David spent most of his mornings, caring for and watering every plant. Along the way, Sarain thought of how she would tell him that she planned to go back to Shaven, but she couldn't imagine a way or an outcome without David becoming upset. It seemed like every day they spent together, the two grew closer, and while Sarain felt as though David had become one of her dearest friends, she suspected that he saw her as much more than that.

Sure enough, as Sarain approached the garden, she right away spotted David harvesting the freshly ripened tomatoes. He smiled when he looked up and saw Sarain approaching, but when he noticed the serious expression upon her face, his smile immediately faded, and he quickly asked, "What's wrong?" Sarain hesitated to answer for a moment, still trying to build up the courage to tell David. "Is the baby okay?" he anxiously asked. "The baby's fine," she abruptly replied, and then cautiously continued by saying, "…but I think it's time for me to leave." David stared at her with confusion, and then he asked, "Did someone say something to you? Are you worried how they're going to react to your pregnancy?" "No, it's nothing like that," Sarain stated, "It's just… Winston." David's eye went wide, and he immediately replied, "Sarain, he's no good for you! He nearly got me killed!" "You don't know him like I do," she noted, "We've been through so much together, and I know he needs me now." "Sarain, you have to think about the safety of your child," David urged. "Winston would never hurt me," she stated, with David still not feeling very assured.

He took a deep breath, while taking a few steps away from Sarain, as though trying to collect his thoughts before he finally turned to her and said, "You're going to be showing soon…" Sarain nodded, and wondered where David was going with his sudden nervous rambling. "And I…I think we should tell the monks that the baby is mine… I'll tell them that we lied about being siblings out of fear of me being excommunicated," David stated timidly. "That could get you into a lot of trouble, David," Sarain quickly replied, "You don't need to do that for me." "No, I want to," he responded, and then he took Sarain by the hand as he stated, "I'll raise this child with you, if you'll have me." Sarain smiled softly up at David, and gave his hand a slight squeeze as she replied, "Oh David, had I met you in another life, I believe you could have made me very happy… But I love Winston, and he needs my help."

David sighed with disappointment, but after a moment he spoke again by saying, "Then I'll go with you." Sarain shook her head, and told him, "No, I'm not willing to put you in harm's way. Winston has already targeted you once before, I can't risk him seeing you as a threat again." "So are you telling me that this is goodbye then?" David asked. Still holding his hand, Sarain gave it another squeeze, and replied, "It is, for now." She began to look away from David, and her grip on his hand loosened until he suddenly gave her a light tug, and said, "If things don't work out how you hope, I want you to remember that you can always come back here." Sarain looked up at David again, as he told her, "My offer will still stand." She smiled at him, and squeezed his hand once more before finally letting it go. She made a motion as though she was going to turn and leave, but then she stopped herself. Sarain looked back up at David, staring into his saddening gray eyes, and then stretched up, placing a hand against his cheek, and her lips gently against his. The kiss only lasted a few seconds, and was merely a soft touch of their lips, but for David, it was an experience like no other in his life, and he knew that he would wait for Sarain to return, regardless of how long it would take or if it would ever even happen.

Sarain left David alone in the garden she had found him in, walking away without another word, or another glance. Each stride away from him she took was stretched long and taken fast, because Sarain knew that if she lingered any longer that she might find herself wanting to change her mind about leaving.

And Winston needed her…more.

Chapter 25

Sarain had packed her few belongings and left quickly that day, walking to a nearby town and taking the first bus she could get that would bring her closer to Shaven. It would take her three days of constant bus rides: four bus changes, and two nights of sleeping at bus stations before Sarain would find herself stepping foot in Shaven again. The small town had become very familiar to Sarain now, and arriving back to it almost felt like coming home, but it was the worried thoughts in the back of Sarain's mind that kept her from feeling excited to be back. Her thoughts and concerns were all about Winston; would he be worse than he was when she left, would he be with Alorea, would he even still be in Shaven?

It was already near dusk as Sarain left the bus station, and quickly started trekking to Winston's house in Wormwood Alley. She carried her backpack on her back and wore her ankh around her neck, and both bounced with every hurried step she took. She chose to take the longer deserted dirt path, rather than the shortcut through the market place so that she wouldn't risk catching someone's eye or being recognized; she recalled being told how her energy was like a beacon to some creatures, and with all her recent training, she had felt that her power to heal had only grown more since that day the tall golden eyed demon-man had attacked her.

Sarain wondered what state she would find Winston in as his house came into view, and she felt both scared and anxious to find out. The sun was starting to set, but Sarain didn't fear it, not with Winston likely to be near. As she approached the house she noticed right away that the door hung open, and was off one of its hinges. Her heart started to race, as she quickly moved through the door. She immediately saw the furniture in shambles, and the walls and floors covered with splatters of black blood. It was obvious that a struggle had occurred, and that someone with demonic blood had been severely injured if not killed.

"Winston!" Sarain immediately shouted, without thinking, and began running down the hallway to check the rest of the rooms for any sign of him. The bathroom was empty, and appeared untouched, but the bedroom was torn to shreds. The mattress had been clawed up, with fluff and springs tossed around the room. The dresser was on its side with all its drawers having been ripped out and smashed. Sarain didn't know what to think, it almost looked like a robbery gone bad, but in a secluded and secret neighborhood for demons? Whatever it was, Sarain was now in a panic over Winston, and knew that it was no longer safe to stay there. She also knew that this meant Winston was likely not coming back, but she worried now about whether he was safe or even alive.

Sarain wondered if this was what her mother had tried to warn her about in her dream, but as she stared again at the black blood sprayed around the living room, she realized that it had to be older than a few days; it had already dried into all the surfaces it stained. Nothing felt wet, not even the porous fabric on the sofa, and the smell of blood only lingered faintly in the air as though it was stale and old. Sarain wondered if this had happened right after she had left town, and she wondered if she could have stopped it if she hadn't.

It had grown completely dark out now, and Sarain knew that she had to seek shelter somewhere else. She had wanted to grab a memento of Winston's, something for her child to have of its father's in case she were to never find or see him again, but there was nothing left in the house that seemed remotely dear to or reminding of Winston. He kept no photos or trinkets, in fact it appeared that he had been living his life like Sarain, with very little that he couldn't do without if ever he had to pick up and leave in a moment's notice.

Sarain sighed, feeling even more defeated than she had before. She thought of where she would go next, where Winston might think to go, and went for the door, but stopped short when she saw the figures of two beings moving toward her direction. They looked like men, but the sudden glow of their eyes when they acknowledged her presence told her otherwise. Sarain took off running, not wanting to go back into the house and allow herself to get cornered in a place that had already failed to protect someone else recently. The vil sangs chased after her, and Sarain began to head towards town, knowing that it would be easier to find safety in the public eye.

Lucky for her, vil sangs were the slower of the demonic kind, and only ran about as fast as Sarain was running now; with her athletic shape, and her not being further into her pregnancy, she still moved as fast and as well as any mortal hunter could move. With her head start, Sarain had faith that she could make it into town before tiring out and slowing down. What she was curious about was whether or not these vil sangs would stop once she had entered a populated domain; if they had been merely out hunting for a meal, then they likely would abandon their pursuit of her, but if these demons knew who she was, then being in the public eye might not stop them.

Sarain raced through the desert, jumping over rocks, and weaving past cacti. The sky loomed clear and starry, and under different circumstances, Sarain would have seen it as a beautiful night. Instead Sarain was making her way into the outskirts of town, and as she did so, she glanced behind her to see that the vil sangs were still in pursuit. This didn't surprise her much though; this part of town was usually unoccupied at any hour, and her target was just a few blocks away where a small shopping center stood. She made a turn down a small street, ran a few yards, and then quickly turned down an alleyway once she realized that the vil sangs had fallen behind. Sarain began to weave through different back alleys, hoping to confuse the vil sangs, who would likely expect her to run a clear shot. Soon Sarain noticed that she was no longer being pursued, and she allowed herself to slow down, and catch her breath. She kept her eyes scanning her surroundings, not trusting her luck with how easily she had lost the vil sangs; it was possible that they had lost interest in her, or that they were newer and weaker for their kind, but it was also possible that they had found another way to trap and catch Sarain.

She treaded carefully, and planned to continue to the normally populated shopping center nearby, just in case. Sarain started to turn down yet another small and usually deserted road, when suddenly and out of nowhere, a figure popped out in front of her, and nearly collided into Sarain. She froze quickly, and stopped herself from reacting as a hunter would, when she realized that the figure was that of a child no more than nine or ten years old. A young girl stood before her, also looking surprised by the almost run-in. The girl had been running in a hurry and with a slight look of panic still on her face, she muttered, "Sorry." Sarain suspected the girl was running late for some kind of curfew, and simply smiled at the child and nodded, then continued on her own way.

Sarain trotted down the street, a little slower now, but it wasn't long before she came upon another disturbance to her trek; she heard the sound of heavy metal music blaring first, before seeing a red old muscle car come blazing around the corner. It narrowly missed hitting Sarain as it weaved down the road, and the driver blasted his horn as though Sarain had been the one at fault, while walking on the sidewalk. She shook her head with annoyance, and began again with her trek when she abruptly heard the sound of tires skidding, followed by a loud thump. Sarain turned around to see the same red muscle car peeling off quickly, leaving behind a large object lying in the road. It took her only a moment to realize that the object was the same girl she had almost collided with moments earlier.

Sarain immediately raced over to the girl, and knelt down by her side. The girl's eyes were closed while blood trickled out of her mouth and nose. Sarain quickly searched the child for a pulse, finding only a very faint beat while pressing her hand against the girl's neck. Sarain then moved her hands to the girl's torso; placing one over the girl's heart, and the other over what felt like broken and caved in ribs. She focused her thoughts, and in her mind she pictured the girl's ribs being pieced back together. Sarain felt her own body grow cold as her hands grew hot, and then she could feel the girl's ribcage begin to form and protrude out as it should. She next envisioned organs healing from puncture wounds made by the girl's once collapsed ribcage. Soon the child's body felt as though it was right once again to Sarain, but the hand that was placed over the girl's heart couldn't feel much of anything; the girl's heart still felt weak.

Sarain scanned her thoughts on what she should do next, but all she could think about was how a defibrillator was used to restart a heart, and she wasn't sure that her healing ability was capable of such a feat. Sarain instead tried to picture making the heart beat as she had done with David, but every time she stopped, the girl's pulse slowed to a crawl.

"Ugh!" Sarain grunted with frustration. She couldn't lose this girl, not after having been able to heal the damage that had been done by the hit and run. It didn't make sense to Sarain, there had to be something left that she could do. She tilted the girl's head back, and started performing CPR, hoping that could do something for the girl that her healing ability hadn't, but after a while of doing so nothing had changed. The girl's heartbeat had slowed even more now, and Sarain doubted that she would have time to get the girl medical care. "Damn it!" Sarain cried out then she placed both of her hands on top of the young girl's chest, took a deep breath, and with one last attempt, pictured a ball of energy being hurdled directly into the girl's heart. Sarain's hands grew almost fiery hot, and as she opened her eyes and gazed down, she saw that her hands were glowing red as though a light was shining from inside them. Sarain gasped, and the glowing energy suddenly shot into the girl's chest. She watched as it appeared to make the child's heart illuminate through her skin. After a few moments the light dissipated, but it was followed by the girl suddenly coughing.

The girl opened her eyes and stared up at Sarain with confusion, and then she asked, "What happened?" Sarain gazed down at the child for a while before responding, "You slipped while dodging a speeding car, and hit your head...But I think you're going to be okay... You should hurry home though." The girl nodded, and Sarain helped her get up on her feet.

She scurried away quickly without another word, but Sarain felt compelled to follow the girl home, just in case. She kept to the shadows while staying a ways behind so as not to alert the girl of her presence. The child's home was only a couple of blocks away from where the car had hit her, and when the girl arrived at her house, instead of being greeted by angry or disappointed parents for her lateness, her parents both appeared worried and relieved to see their child. Sarain was glad to see that the girl had made it home safely, and she knew that that would have been impossible without her efforts to save the child's life.

Sarain smiled to herself, realizing that she was able to still save lives without her demonic strength. She looked down at her stomach, thinking of the other thing she was now capable of doing that she couldn't before. Sarain sighed, feeling tired from having used so much energy to heal the girl. She glanced around at her surroundings, still spying no signs of the vil sangs that had chased her earlier.

"They must have been looking for an easier meal," Sarain thought to herself, and with that, she felt it safe to skip going to the shopping center to seek safety in public. Besides, Sarain was feeling exhausted now, and wanted a place to rest her head. She didn't trust the town's hotel, anyone who could be looking for her would easily find her there; the only place she did trust, knowing its secluded location, was Orran's old safe house.

The walk to Orran's place would be a long one for Sarain that night, not necessarily because of the distance, but because of how tired she found herself growing; healing that girl had taken a lot out of her. Sarain thought of what she would do next, and where Winston might go if he was still alive. If he had survived the scuffle that appeared to have taken place in his home, she figured that he would have likely left town, not only out of safety, but also possibly in search of her. She wondered if he would be with Alorea or if he had finally come to his senses about her. Perhaps the time apart would have given

Winston better perspective over his relationship with Sarain, but then she worried that he could have gotten worse, not only out of grief, but from Aion's blood.

Sarain also feared that she wouldn't find Winston; not only could he be dead, but it was also possible that he wouldn't want Sarain to find him. She had broken his heart by leaving once before, having left again might have been too much for Winston to handle. It was very feasible that Sarain would never see Winston again, and with that thought, she wondered if she should just return back to the monastery, where she and her unborn child would be safe and David would be waiting. Sarain hoped that some rest would bring her clarity, and that perhaps tomorrow, with the protection of daylight, she could find some trace or answer to what had become of Winston.

Finally Sarain began to make her way through the densely wooded area that surrounded Orran's old safe house. The trees blocked out the light of the moon, making it dark and hard for Sarain to see. She took her steps carefully so not to trip and fall, and she had to go off of the memory of how to get to the safe house, as though she were blind. After a slow and cautious trek, Sarain at last saw the structure of the safe house come into sight. With moonlight peering through the small clearing, her eyes immediately focused on the house, and then scanned the heavily grassy ground to where Orran's gravesite stood. Sarain almost felt herself wanting to smile as though she was about to be reunited with her friend, or at least the memories of their final days together, which felt so vivid in this location.

Sarain saw the tip of his wooden grave marker peeking through the tall grass, and there was something about the sight of this that caused her to stop in her tracks. Strangely, though she had visited her friend's grave once before, this time she suddenly felt full of dread. It was a feeling that had appeared seemingly out of nowhere, but it was one that Sarain did not take lightly; in her experience, her gut feelings had proven accurate and ominous in some way. But knowing that only she and Winston had knowledge of this place made her doubt her sudden strange feeling; still she hesitantly took another step forward. With that step she felt a wave of oddly warm air rush towards her, though there was no wind moving the trees on this cool night.

Sarain stopped again, now feeling overwhelmed with emotions that seemed to have come with the strangely warm breeze, and something about it felt familiar. With no real explanation as to why, she suddenly began to turn around as though to leave, with another warm breeze pushing against her back as if urging her to go. It was when Sarain heard the snapping of a twig that she immediately felt a chill go down her spine, and then the wind picked up more, this time cold. It howled through the trees, whirling until it sounded like wailing, and with it came a voice whispering, "Run" with a sound of urgency to its tone. The voice seemed to be formed from the wind itself and it brought tears to Sarain's eyes as she recognized it to be that of her departed friend, Orran.

Chapter 26

Sarain did as the disembodied voice of her friend told her, and began to run, hearing movement quickly following from behind her. She prayed she wouldn't trip as she rushed through the heavily wooded and cluttered forest, and she also prayed that she wouldn't find out what it was that she could clearly hear chasing behind her.

Sarain raced with her heart thumping and exhaustion already setting in from having never had a chance to recoup from the events earlier in the night. She could feel her pace slowing even though she pressed her burning leg muscles to continue on. She frightfully heard what sounded like, not only one, but several sounds of leaves and twigs crunching, coming from multiple angles behind her. Her breathing became heavy, almost masking the growls that were nearing behind her.

It was the moment that Sarain felt her foot slip that her heart nearly stopped. A mound of moss slid under her shoe, causing her to lose traction with her speed, and she began to fall forward towards a heap of thorny vines. Time seemed to move at a crawl as she saw the rugged ground moving slowly closer. She brought her arms out, hoping to break her fall, but gasped when she didn't collide into the ground. Instead, she felt the firm grips of clawed hands on her arms, and soon she was being raised into the air. Sarain lifted her head up and looked back at her captors to see three demonic beasts carrying her: one holding onto each arm and the third holding up her legs. For a moment Sarain tried to struggle, but with her exhaustion, she knew it was futile. Then she realized as the demons continued to carry her that they were not simply looking for a quick meal, but instead were taking her to somewhere else altogether.

Sarain wondered if she was to be a meal for something else, but suspected that these seemingly animalistic beasts actually comprehended enough to know who she was. They were definitely taking her somewhere specific, and possibly to someone. As she hung her head, waiting for the creatures to get her to their final destination, she wondered what was in store for her; was she to be sacrificed, did these creatures know of the energy that Sarain possessed, or was this about vengeance for killing Aion. Sarain wondered if these were the beasts that made the carnage that she had found at Winston's, and then she wondered if they had killed him. She felt herself getting angrier the more she thought about it, as her concern for her own wellbeing dwindled. Sarain's only worry for herself was actually for the welfare of her unborn child, which she was sure that the beasts wouldn't be able to sense at this point, but any harm that would come to her would likely put her child's life at risk, and of course if she were to die, her child would leave this world with her.

Sarain didn't know what she should do, or could do for that matter. Even if these beasts allowed her to live long enough for her to muster the energy to fight, she no longer had the strength to take on multiple demons. Her only chance was to hope that the beasts let her live another day, because then with time she could recoup her energy and try to escape while the beasts slept or were at least weakened by the day. Sarain knew that these were likely empty hopes and dreams, and all that she could really do now was to wait; wait to see what they had planned for her.

It took nearly an hour for the three creatures to carry Sarain to their destination, but she knew it immediately when they came upon the cavernous mountainside where the Brotherhood headquarters had been.

This had to be about Aion; about killing their leader and blowing up their sanctuary, Sarain thought to herself. She wondered if they planned to kill her at the top of the mountain where she had died once before, and she wondered if there were others waiting to take their vengeance on her when they arrived.

When they were about halfway up the mountainside, Sarain noticed that the beasts that carried her turned in the wrong direction, or at least didn't appear to be taking her up the path to get to the peak of the mountain. Instead, they headed to where the opening to the cavern had once been, and then to Sarain's amazement, she saw that it now stood open again.

"We blew that up," she muttered with shock, remembering how, with the explosion, the cave had collapsed upon itself. Without having been told, she realized that the beasts that had fled that night must have come back, dug open, and rebuilt the Brotherhood's headquarters in the time that had passed since that fateful night. Sarain felt her heart drop to the pit of her stomach. If the demons had enough manpower to rebuild their lair, then killing her father, losing Orran, and dying herself had stopped nothing but just a few mad men, which likely had already been replaced with new ones.

They continued to carry Sarain into the cavern, which without the light of the moon and stars, was a mass of darkness, and without demonic blood, Sarain lacked the ability to see in the dark as she once had. The air was cold, and grew colder the deeper down they took her. She felt the beasts twist and turn through the labyrinth that was their lair, and wasn't sure where it was that they were taking her, but she could sense that it was far below where they had started. The air felt thin as Sarain finally saw light once again; candles dimly lit the way now, and sounds of scuffling and muffled growls caught her attention. She lifted her head up to see that the narrow cavern passage had opened into a large corridor where many other demons lay waiting, and amongst them were a mixture of full-blooded demons, demonic vil sangs, and vil sangs that still looked human. Strangely, there was no fighting or segregation among them and unlike what she was used to, they all appeared to hold each other as equals. What she also noticed was that all their eyes were ablaze and focused on her. A lot of the creatures stared at her with expressions of hate on their faces, while more of the vil sangs, likely the more newly made, gazed upon her with awe and curiosity.

Sarain felt the beasts that carried her come to an abrupt stop, and they began to lower her until she was placed on the cold, hard, stone ground and on all fours as though she were an animal. She remained there, still, for a moment, unsure what was in store for her, and not wanting to do anything that would cause all her onlookers to react. Sarain slowly lifted her head to see a pair of large black boots in front of her, and she realized that the beasts had placed her at the foot of someone who appeared to be sitting on a throne carved into the stone.

They have a new leader, Sarain thought to herself, and then she let her eyes slowly wander up to look upon her captor. She saw that his clawed hands gripped the throne's armrests firmly, with his thick black nails nearly digging into the stone. His skin had a bluish gray hue, and looked hard, almost scaly. He had a bulky, muscular figure, and had a humanoid shape that told her that this had once been a human man. With fear beating through Sarain, she finally mustered the courage to look upon the face of the new Brotherhood leader. His ears were pointed, his long hair was white, and his eyes were the same shade of violet that hers had once been.

"Oh god," Sarain cried out, with tears falling from her eyes. He flinched as though shuddering from her response to him, but to his amazement, he saw a weak smile spread across her tear stained face. "You're alive, Winston…" she affirmed with a smile, and tears rolling off her cheeks.

Chapter 27

"What are you doing here?" Sarain asked, while moving towards a demonic-looking Winston, but she was suddenly stopped when two demons standing nearby quickly rushed over and grabbed her by her arms, holding her back from him.

"Hands off your queen!" Winston immediately shouted, his eyes afire, and the beasts abruptly let go of her. Sarain stared at Winston in disbelief, already knowing what he was about to say; "I am their new king."

"Are you crazy? We fought to destroy them!" Sarain spoke astounded. "They are not the same beasts they once were. With me they are united, docile, and intelligent. They only feed when necessary, and they only feed on the scum that won't be missed," Winston stated. "Docile, really? They attacked me in the woods, and outside your house," she replied. "No, they didn't, they were instructed to keep an eye out for you, in case you one day decided to come back to me. Which I am pleased to see that you have, and they brought you here unharmed, didn't they?" Winston proclaimed with certainty.

Sarain glanced around at the horde of demons gathered in the room, and then she stated, "Many of them are glaring at me." "Well you did kill their last leader, but don't worry, I won't let any harm come to you," Winston responded, and then added, "They know that you are to be my bride, and their queen." Sarain turned back to him, and remarked, "This isn't you, Winston." "Can you not see what I am while standing right in front of me?" Winston asked firmly, and stated, "I am more beast now than man! I have fed on blood the entire time you have known me, and have you forgotten how we met?"

Sarain was quiet, a bit stunned, as she listened to him say, "I helped build an army before, and I was good at it!" "But this dream of yours won't last, they're wild and evil, and it's only a matter of time before they go back to chaos," she rebutted. "They are the same as me, and as you once were….and as you will be again," he announced. "What?" Sarain muttered, appalled. "Did you think they would have a queen that wasn't one of them?" Winston asked, and explained, "Sarain, this way we'll be together for all eternity, and we'll have an army behind us."

Sarain gasped, thinking of her unborn child, and knowing that it would likely not survive if she were to be turned into a vil sang. But as Sarain searched for some way to reply, she found herself holding back from telling Winston about his child. Surely the news would get him to stall turning her, but at the same time it would bring into question how she was able to become pregnant with his child, which worried her that he would either assume it wasn't his, or more importantly, find out about the ability she came back with. And Sarain knew that her healing ability was her last chance of getting the old Winston back. She just hoped that she had enough power to undo what her father's blood had done to him, or at least bring him to his senses.

"So what do you say?" Winston asked her curiously. Sarain took a deep breath, and replied, "When's the wedding?" Winston smiled, his fangs protruding out his mouth, and answered, "As soon as possible. I'll start planning the ceremony; we'll be wed, and then you'll be turned."

Sarain felt her stomach churn, as though her unborn child knew what was in store. And her nerves tensed as the countdown began.

A short time later, Sarain found herself sitting in a candle lit room alone, having been led there by a demon ordered to by Winston, who had promised to come visit her once he was done talking to his legion.

The room reminded her of the one Aion had kept her in during her last stay there, but this one didn't appear to have a lock on the door, and Sarain wondered if this was because Winston trusted her, or if it was because the room was already heavily guarded outside the door. She didn't have to wait long before the door opened, and the demonic-looking Winton stepped in, barely fitting through the doorway, having become bigger and taller than he had been a month earlier when she had left him.

"I hope you like the accommodations, I had it set up just for you," he stated. "This isn't your room?" she asked. "No, I had them set you up with your own, so we can keep at least one wedding tradition," he replied. Sarain let her gaze fall upon the floor, causing Winston to remark, "I want you to get used to living here; this is your home now. You're not a prisoner, you're free to leave this room and roam around the headquarters, I just ask that you don't leave the cavern."

Sarain then stared up at Winston and said, "Can't we just leave here together? We're alone now, you can tell me, this can't be what you really want." "But it is. Sarain, this way we have nothing to fear, and you finally get your wish for stopping the evil ways of demons," he responded. "The only thing that's going to change is you and me," she replied. Winston sighed disappointedly, and after a moment of hesitation, he asked, "Do you still love me? Can you love me as I am now?"

Sarain stared back up at him, studying his new demonic features, and then she reached over and took his cold, clawed hand with hers, and intertwined her tanned human fingers in between his. "You'll always be beautiful to me," she told him. A small smile formed on his face, but Sarain noticed a hint of doubt in Winston's eyes. She then stood up, still holding onto Winston's hand, and stretched up as far as the tips of her toes would allow her. With her free hand she caressed his cheek, bringing his face down to hers, and kissed him gently on his lips. After a second to get past his surprise, Winston began to kiss Sarain back, pulling her closer to him. He could feel his passion for her begin to burn, and as he started to kiss her more lustfully he suddenly felt her flinch.

Winston pulled away to see Sarain bring her hand up to her lip where she wiped away a drop of blood, and he realized that he had accidentally cut her with one of his fangs. Winston immediately pushed Sarain away, and then after taking a good long look at her, he said, as if coming to some kind of realization, "No, you can't possibly still love me, not like this, not with how much you hate demons." "Winston," she said with a worried tone, but he stopped her before she could say anymore. "You left me so many times before… But it doesn't matter, you won't be able to leave me again," he stated with a firm and somewhat infuriated tone, "You will be at my side, as my queen, whether you want to or not!"

Winston then stormed out of the room, slamming the door behind him. Sarain stood there in shock for a while, before finally managing to sit down on the bed. Her eyes began to well up as she grasped that the Winston she had known was fading away, and she cried realizing that her fate was likely sealed.

Chapter 28

Sarain spent the next couple of days holed up in her room, with only silent demons bringing her food and water stopping by. While she was alone, she practiced her healing ability, and she spent the remaining time resting and building up her strength. Sarain tried to think of a way to get Winston alone and away from the other demons; it'd be the only way for her to use her ability on him safely enough to where she wouldn't have to worry about anyone interfering, but with Winston not letting her leave the cavern, there was no place that didn't have a demon guard nearby.

Sarain's thoughts were interrupted when the door opened, and a vil sang woman stepped in. Sarain stared at her curiously, this being the first time she had seen her and also being a bit surprised that the woman hadn't knocked like the other demons had done before. The woman had long auburn hair, and wore clothes that looked too tight for her body. Sarain suspected that this woman was a newer made vil sang, since she still cared about her appearance by wearing lots of makeup.

The woman held a firm gaze on Sarain, and she smirked as she stated, "The King wants you to join him in the main hall." Without a word, Sarain got up from the bed with a sigh, and followed the woman out of the room. As they walked down the narrow hallway, Sarain noticed that the woman walked with a sway and arched her back as if trying to show off her womanly assets. When they arrived, Sarain recognized that they were in the same corridor that she had been brought to on her first night there. Sitting at his throne was Winston, whom she hadn't seen since that first night, and gathered around him were a variety of demons, all listening to his every word.

Winston looked up as Sarain entered the room, and with a smile, he said, "Ah, there's my beautiful bride." Sarain gave him a perplexed look, wondering if he was still doubting her love for him. "Come here, dear, we were just discussing the wedding ceremony." Sarain walked over, and with a slightly sarcastic tone, asked, "And how do demons throw a wedding?" Winston ignored her tone, and replied, "Much the same as mortals would; you'll get to wear a gown, we'll be surrounded by onlookers, but instead of simply exchanging vows, we'll exchange blood." "Do I get any say in the arrangements?" she asked solemnly. "If you were hoping to nix the blood, then no," he replied smugly. Sarain gazed at him firmly, as she spoke, "I understand that there's no talking you out of turning me, but you can at least grant me a private wedding. I don't want to spend my final moments of humanity with a bunch of demons." Winston sighed, and then stated, "They want to see and celebrate as you become one of us, Sarain," but when he saw the disappointment in her eyes, he quickly added, "but I'll think about it." The answer wasn't exactly promising, but it was all Sarain could hope for: a true moment alone with Winston.

"In the meantime, I would like to see you up and about from your room. You should get to know your future family," Winston instructed, and then he turned to one of the large demons near him, and started discussing hunting and feeding schedules. Sarain sighed, realizing that Winston's request for her presence was more about integrating her in with his army than actually seeing her.

Sarain took a step back, and she stood alone near a wall. She watched as Winston delegated orders, fitting the role of a ruler well, and she noticed that every once in a while he glanced up and in her direction. She wasn't sure if this was to see if she was mingling or if he just wanted to see her. Sarain scanned the room with her eyes, finding it strange to be in a place where so many demons stood, and not being attacked. It was even stranger yet to see them all talking and interacting with one another like normal people do. Given the marketplace had a mixture of demons and people that frequented it, there was still always a level of tension there; but here, in this room, Winston really had managed to make the demons seem more docile. Either way, Sarain wasn't in a hurry to join them.

She watched a while longer, until her eyes settled on the vil sang woman that had retrieved her earlier. The woman had an intense look on her face, and Sarain followed her gaze to see that she was staring intently at Winston. He didn't return her glances, but the stare still concerned Sarain, because she was sure that the expression on the woman's face was one of lust. All her years of hunting and watching people had taught Sarain a thing or two about reading the body language of people, and recalling how the vil sang woman had looked at her earlier now made sense; she saw her as a rival.

A moment later, a vil sang man came up next to Sarain, breaking her concentration on the woman, when he remarked, "I see you noticed Kara's infatuation with the king." Sarain glanced at the vil sang, who could easily pass as a mortal man, and replied, "Well she does make it pretty obvious." "She's had her eye on him since he arrived; she couldn't have been happy to hear that you came back in town," he stated, and then smirked as he said, "But I'm glad that she won't be getting her way; she'd make a terrible queen." "Could she really be worse than a queen who's spent her life hunting your kind?" Sarain muttered back. The vil sang man looked her in the face, and replied, "Yes, because at least you have conviction; Kara doesn't care about anything other than herself, and she couldn't lead herself out of a paper bag."

Sarain let out a small chuckle, then looked away from the vil sang man, returning her gaze back up in time to see Winston staring over in her direction, a stern look upon his face. Sarain returned Winston's gaze, and watched intently as he ordered, "Kara, take Sarain back to her room." The auburn haired vixen moved quickly to follow her master's order, and grabbed Sarain by the arm in doing so. She pulled her down the hallway, where Sarain abruptly yanked her arm away, and stated, "I can find my own way there," but Kara followed her back to her room anyway.

When they got inside, Sarain turned to Kara and remarked, "Well, I'm here, and he said nothing about you staying, so go!" Kara sneered and then muttered, "I really don't know what he sees in you; you're certainly not prettier than me." "I guess he prefers women that don't have to hide behind a pile of makeup," Sarain retorted. Kara scowled at Sarain, letting out a deep, low growl, before slamming the door behind her.

Sarain scoffed, half amused by the naïve vil sang's jealousy, and then she sat down on the bed, thinking of Winston. It seemed like he questioned her every move, and the more the demonic blood took over him, the more he pulled away from her. Sarain wondered if this meant that he would eventually tire of her or grow to hate her. She shook her head, and reminded herself that her goal was to get the old Winston back, but her thoughts kept continuing to drift to if she couldn't save Winston. Sarain didn't think she had either the strength or the will to kill him; her only chance for survival would be to run, for both her and her unborn child's sake. Sarain knew that her deadline would be the wedding ritual; she just had to convince Winston to make it private.

Just then her door creaked open, and Winston slowly stepped in. Sarain looked over, a little surprised to see him, and asked, "What was that all about? I thought you wanted me to get to know your followers." Winston glanced away from her gaze, and muttered, "I didn't think about how the vil sang men might respond to you, especially with more men around here than women." "You were jealous, because I talked to that guy?" Sarain observed. "I was jealous that he made you laugh," he replied. "Winston, you have nothing to worry about, I'm not about to betray you by taking up with some vil sang," she spoke reassuringly. "I wish that I could believe that, but with my features growing more and more demonic, it only makes sense that you would be attracted elsewhere," he solemnly said. "Damn it, Winston," Sarain harked with annoyance, "if anyone has to be worried, then it is me with that damn Kara trying to catch your eye!" "Kara?" he astounded. "Yes, Kara, with her eagerness to serve you, and her comments on how much more attractive she thinks she is compared to me. And it's not like she'd be the first woman to try and come between us, in fact where is your little friend, Alorea?" Sarain stated with a sharp tongue. "Alorea is dead; punishment for wanting to hurt you," Winston snapped back firmly to Sarain's astonishment, and further remarked, "And as for Kara, I will make sure she understands where she ranks compared to you."

Winston turned and left without another word, leaving Sarain stunned by his coldness.

Sarain cradled her newborn child with sweat still clinging to her brow, a tear rolling down her cheek as she smiled upon her beautiful baby boy, who slept soundly in her arms. He stirred and began to coo as Sarain gazed lovingly at him, and she softly spoke, "Are you hungry, sweetheart?"

Sarain maneuvered so that she could nurse her child when she was stopped by a voice saying, "He doesn't want that." Sarain looked up towards the voice to see a demonic Winston standing by her side. "He needs to eat," she weakly muttered, but Winston simply shook his head and replied, "Let me feed our son." Then she watched as he took one of his long sharp claws to his own wrist and slit it open like a knife into butter. Black blood poured out of the wound as Winston began to reach for his child. Sarain clung to her son tightly as she cried out, "No, I don't want that life for our son!"

Winston then paused, no longer moving to grab the infant, but instead gazed down at Sarain and said, "It's too late; my blood already beats through his veins." "No, he's human like me," she insisted. Winston extended a clawed, pointed finger towards the infant, and said, "Look closer at our child." Sarain stared down at the cooing baby, and watched as he opened his eyes and peered up at her with the same shade of violet that she knew so well.

Sarain shook her head furiously, crying out, "No, I had decades before I fully turned, I can save him!" But she observed in dismay as the child began to cry out in hunger with a pair of small fangs poking out from his mouth. "Nooooo!" she screamed in agony as she watched Winston take the tiny demon from her arms. He cradled his son lovingly as he brought his bloody wrist up to the baby's hungry lips.

"That's a good boy, drink up, and become big and strong," Winston spoke proudly to his son, "Because one day you will lead my army."

Sarain suddenly shot up in bed, drenched in sweat, and calling out, "Don't take my baby!" It took her a moment to realize that she had only been dreaming, but it took her only a second more to realize that she wasn't alone.

"Your baby?" an intrigued voice asked. Sarain eyes immediately focused on the badly scarred and bloody face of the vil sang Kara, who was standing beside her bed. "Interesting, does the King know that you stepped out on him and got yourself knocked up?" she said with delight in her voice.

Chapter 29

"Your face," Sarain muttered with disgust. "Ya, it looks like you went whining to your king about me, but I wonder what he'll do to you when he learns about your betrayal?" Kara noted smugly. Sarain's hand immediately went to her chest, and Kara laughed, leaning in with a toothy grin, and saying, "Oh, are you scared of me?" Sarain stared up at the devilish woman, and replied, "I could never fear such a naïve wretch like you, just like I could never betray the love of my life."

Suddenly Sarain leapt forward, ripping the chain from her ankh off her neck as she shoved the pendant into the gaping wound on Kara's face. The vil sang let out a bloodcurdling scream as the sizzling smell of her foul burning flesh invaded Sarain's nose. Kara growled furiously, but Sarain was on her before the vil sang could react further; punching the ankh deeper into her face. Kara screamed again, with her eyes burning wrathfully as she swiftly shoved Sarain back. She then grabbed at her broken and spongy flesh, so desperate to get the ankh off her that she ripped away a chunk of her own cheek to do so.

The vil sang turned to Sarain with hate on her face and she quickly leapt on to her like a cat. Sarain struggled to push the rabid beast off of her, digging her nails deeply into Kara's chest as she used all her strength to keep the crazed woman back. Kara growled and snapped at her, as Sarain maneuvered to bring her legs up between her and her attacker, and once she had succeeded she forcefully kicked the vil snag back and off of her. Kara staggered backward, taking only a moment to recover before moving in to leap on Sarain again. But before she had the chance to retaliate, Kara suddenly found herself unable to move.

Kara felt a tightness around her neck, causing her hands to fly up to try and pry herself free. She tried to see what had taken hold of her with her eyes moving wildly, but the sound of her neck bones cracking and her throat collapsing was all the answer she would find. Soon Kara's lifeless body fell to the floor with a thud as the on-looking Sarain panted trying to catch her breath. She watched as her savior moved toward her, extending his clawed hand to help her up. Sarain took his hand and let him pull her up to her feet where she quickly threw her arms around him and said, "Oh Winston, you got here just in time." He gazed down at the body of his servant on the ground and remarked, "It looks like you were doing fine without me," and gently pushing Sarain away, Winston bent down and retrieved the bloody ankh from the ground, and said, "I'll get this cleaned and fixed, then you should continue to keep it on until you are turned."

Sarain's relief quickly faded, as she realized that nothing had changed in Winston's mind about what was to become of her. He gazed around the room and stated,

"I'll have your things brought to my chamber." "You want me to stay with you?" she quickly remarked. "No, I'll stay elsewhere," he said, and then noted, "But my room is the only one that locks from the inside."

Winston then walked away, ordering servants to clean up the mess and to help Sarain to her new room.

Sarain got moved into her new room, but she didn't really sleep anymore that morning. Instead she spent the hours thinking and reflecting on her life and all the things she had done wrong. She sat on the large bed, knowing that it was where Winston normally slept, and where he planned for them to sleep together once she was turned. Sarain touched the indented pillow and thought of how much she missed sleeping next to Winston. She remembered how he would hold her as they would spend their days in bed, how she would catch him watching her sleep, and how he would kiss the back of her neck when he had thought she was sleeping. She thought of all the years she had lost that she could have spent with him, and even though she had spent those years saving people and killing demons, they suddenly seemed so hollow now knowing what she had missed out on.

Sarain wondered what her life would be like if she failed to break the demonic hold on Winston, and he turned her into a vil sang; given she would likely lose her child, she would at least have Winston by her side for an eternity. But Sarain had spent so many years thinking that she could never have a child, losing her baby now would break her heart, especially knowing that the child was made during the happiest time of their life together.

Sarain desperately wanted both Winston and their child, but it was looking more and more like she would one day have to choose, or else the choice would no longer be hers to make.

Sarain sighed with frustration, she needed to see Winston. His constant efforts to avoid her was making it harder for her to put her plan to work; she had to convince him to take her away from the Brotherhood headquarters for their wedding ritual. She glanced at the door, wondering if he would even be awake at that hour; such strong daylight hours were prime sleeping times for demons. She thought of how he had wanted her to mingle with "their people", and then she decided that she could kill two birds with one stone by going out and looking for him.

Sarain quickly dressed and then unlocked the door. She swung the door open with it heavily groaning, and stepped out into the dimly lit narrow hallway. A few feet from her door stood two demons standing stiffly and clearly on guard. The fierce looking demons had hard shell-like skin and both appeared to have never spent a day as mortals. She hesitantly walked up to one and asked, "Where's the king?" "Main hall," it grunted out in a deep hoarse voice. Sarain took a step back, and began to walk down the long passage towards the main corridor, with the two demons still waiting outside her room, as though guarding to make sure no one else entered it while she was gone.

The tunnels were quiet, with most demons likely slumbering. Sarain's steps echoed with each pace, confirming to herself that escaping stealthily from a ceremony held in the cavern would be next to impossible. As she reached the main corridor, she noticed a few demons were indeed awake and socializing, as humans would, inside. They were mostly the purebred beasts, though a handful were vil sangs, but Sarain quickly noticed that those were only women, and she wondered if Winston had done something to the vil sang men.

Sarain quickly observed that Winston's throne sat empty, and she glanced around to see if he was somewhere in the crowd. One of the creatures took notice of her distress, and approached her cautiously like a cat would to a new owner. He was a towering beast, standing at nearly seven feet, and while he had the shape of a man, the rest of him looked nothing else like one. He had big hard scales, jet black skin, and large yellow eyes, and if he had ever once been a human man, he hadn't been one in a very long time.

"Are you looking for the King?" the beast spoke with a low and bass-y voice. "Yes, I was told that he was in here," Sarain replied. "He was, but he just stepped out," it informed her, and then remarked, "But I can take you to him." She stared up at him, hesitantly, not wanting to trust the demon to lead her off somewhere unknown, especially after the incident with Kara. But then Sarain thought of how Winston wanted her to get to know the demons, and she did want to see him; perhaps this could help convince Winston that he can still trust her.

The reluctant Sarain agreed, and began to follow the demon out of the corridor and down another passageway. This tunnel was less lit, and at times almost pitch black. The walk seemed long, with Sarain wondering all the while where exactly they were going, and why this place was so far from the rest of the Brotherhood's domain. She felt herself growing more and more on guard as she suspected that she had made the wrong decision in trusting to follow this demon. But she kept her concerns quiet, still hoping to be led to Winston in the end.

Soon light began to enter the tunnel once again, but Sarain was surprised to see, once she rounded a corner, that the light wasn't cast by a flame, but instead was flooding in from the entrance of the cave. She stopped in her tracks, and quickly turned and looked at the demon that had led her there, questioning his motives. He stood very still, watching her vigilantly until he finally opened his mouth to say, "I served your father for centuries… He was always a strong and firm ruler, but after he met your mother he changed…and then when he found out about you he became obsessed with finding you…" Sarain stared at the beast, confused as to where he was going with his rant. "You made your father weak, and you make Winston weak too," he concluded, "You are simply the worst thing that has ever happened to the Brotherhood." Sarain knew exactly where this was headed, and she began to speak as she readied herself for the next step, "You blame me for your legion's downfall, but all I'm hearing is the whining of a grunt that is too weak to do anything but follow his master's orders."

The beast tightened his fists and let out a low growl as Sarain continued on by saying, "And what is your big plan now? Are you going to make it look as though I was trying to escape?" "Actually that's exactly what I had in mind," the demon hissed. "Figures, just another weak-minded animal," Sarain scoffed and said, "Like Winston would ever let that be justification for my death." And with that the creature howled, and Sarain took off running towards the cavern's entrance. The beast leapt on all fours, chasing after her like a dog, and Sarain made it halfway to the cave's entrance before she felt the beast's claws scrape against her left shoulder. She stumbled and staggered out of the demon's path just enough to avoid a deadly strike, and as she swiftly turned around to face him, she heard herself scream out as she felt her hands begin to burn. Without thinking, Sarain let out a pulse of energy through her hands and right into the demon, and in a moment that seemed to last a lifetime, she watched as the beast faltered.

He dropped to his knees, his eyes wide with amazement, leading Sarain to believe that she had stunned him, and she took off running, again, for daylight. But unbeknownst to her, she had done much more than simply staggered the beast; what she didn't know and couldn't hear, was the weak heart beat that had started in the demon's chest. The organ had gone unused for centuries and the creature itself had forgotten it had even existed.

After a few seconds, the heart ceased to beat once more, and the beast came to his senses in time to chase after Sarain again. She neared the exit, but before she could reach it, she felt the cold and scaly hands of the demon wrapping around her. The beast went to sink his teeth into Sarain when he too suddenly felt clawed hands on his body, and he threw his head back to see the fiery violet eyes of his king blazing down at him. Winston collided into the demon, causing Sarain to fly forward and out of its grasp.

Winston buried his fangs into the back of the beast who violently swatted at his attacker. After a few attempts, the demon finally managed to knock Winston off of him, but as soon as the king was back on his feet, he was pouncing back onto his faulty servant. The demon howled in pain as Winston bit deeply into the creature's arm, chomping down into his shoulder, and chewing his way to the bone. The beast cried out, and struggled as Winston pinned him, face down, on to the ground. He pressed the demon's face into the dirt, forcefully, causing the beast to choke on mouthfuls of loose earth, before he finally bent down and bit into the creature's jugular, severing it and allowing its black blood to spray across the cavern.

After a second to allow his adrenaline to calm, Winston finally stood back up, and he then thought to check on Sarain's wellbeing. His eyes quickly scanned his surroundings, but it wasn't until he expanded his search that he saw where Sarain stood. She stared over at him, her eyes wide with bewilderment, and if his heart had been able to beat, Winston's would have been racing, when he saw the sun in her hair.

Sarain stood safely in the warmth of the sun, just outside the cavern, watching as Winston was helpless to retrieve her. His eyes burned as he waited for her to walk away, knowing that this was likely to be his last glance of her. Sarain stared on, not sure what to say, but aware that this was her chance at freedom and safety.

Sarain took one last long look at Winston, and then with a deep breath, she took her first step, but not towards freedom. Instead, Sarain found herself stepping back into the cave and towards Winston. He gasped, utterly shocked by her decision, and watched as she approached him, and said, "Take me back to my room."

Chapter 30

Winston immediately ordered his army to gather in the main hall, and after safely escorting Sarain to her room, he stood before the Brotherhood with a fury blazing in his eyes.

"What part of respect and serve your queen, do you all not understand?" he angrily shouted at the beasts. "Aion is dead! The days of you following his rules are over! I'm your leader now, and I will tear out the throat of anyone who so much as even looks at Sarain the wrong way! I have killed countless of our kind for that woman, and I'd have no problem killing anyone else who wrongs her!" Winston began to pace back and forth as he continued, "If you really want to honor Aion, you'd honor his daughter, and you'd bow down to the one who has his blood flowing in his veins." He stopped in his tracks, took a deep breath, and said, "Aion always wanted his daughter to lead his army, and with me, his dream can finally become a reality, as she will rule by my side. You couldn't ask for a stronger leader than someone who has already conquered over so many of our kind before. With that kind of strength we'll be unstoppable!"

"But she cleansed herself of our blood, what's to stop her from doing it again?" a beast called out. "That only proves how strong and capable she is!" Winston replied, "She has done something no other being has ever done before, and this time she will accept our blood willingly! This shows us that she is finally ready to lead you all!"

Some of the beasts cheered, while others still held their doubts, but didn't question their king. Winston worried about the loyalty of his army, but did his best not to show it. He just prayed that his words would be enough to ensure Sarain's safety from then on.

Sarain paced around the room, wondering if she had made the right decision in staying with Winston. She thought of how good it had felt to feel the sun warming her skin as she stood in the daylight just outside the cavern's entrance, but when she had seen that look of fear in Winston's eyes, she realized that she felt that same fear reflected in herself when she thought of a life without him.

Sarain knew that her chances of getting Winston safely away from the Brotherhood were slim, and with his appearance becoming more demonic, any life they would have together would have to be spent in hiding. Though even with all this in consideration, she still couldn't leave him, and she began to wonder what would happen if she told Winston about the baby. Would he believe her? Would he accuse her of cheating? Would he allow her to carry the child to term before turning her? Was it even possible to raise a child amongst demons?

Sarain felt unsure about everything, almost missing the days when all her problems could be solved by fighting. She sighed just before a knock came to the door. She stared over at the door for a second before she heard Winston say, "It's me Sarain," from the other side. She quickly went and unlatched the lock so that she could open the door for Winston. He stood there, looking massive, on the other side of the doorway. Sarain stepped back to give him room to walk in, and he lowered his head so that he could get in through the room's arch framed entrance. She immediately shut the door behind Winston, latching it once again, not wanting to have to deal with any demon other than him.

Sarain turned to Winston, just in time to hear him ask, "How are you feeling? Are you alright?" She shifted her left shoulder awkwardly, and replied, "I think he scraped my shoulder, it's been sore since the scuffle." Winston moved in to give Sarain's shoulder a quick glance, but was caught off guard when she suddenly took off her shirt so that he could get a better look at the wound. She turned around, and moved her hair to the side, exposing both her shoulder and her neck to Winston. He was surprised to see that Sarain still trusted and treated him the same even though his appearance was now very demonic. He lifted his bluish gray-clawed hand and gently traced over the freshly scabbed claw marks on Sarain's back.

"It's already healing," he told her, and Sarain immediately turned around to face Winston as she asked, "How are you? Did he hurt you at all?" Winston stared down at Sarain as she glanced him over for any injuries; he studied her tanned skin and admired her bare breasts while she was busy checking him for wounds. Sarain's eyes settled upon what appeared to be a couple of small droplets of black blood on Winston's shirt. Unsure of whether or not the blood was his, Sarain abruptly began unbuttoning Winston's shirt to check, catching him off guard again. She scanned his gray skin until she spotted the source of the blood at the top of Winston's abs. She placed her hand to the wound with Winston's skin nearly feeling like ice. The cut was still damp, but not big, it looked as though the beast had managed to insert one of his claws directly into Winston; making the wound deep but not wide.

"Does it hurt?" Sarain asked with concern, trying to focus her energy to her hands in hopes of healing the wound without thinking of how Winston might react. But instead of answering Sarain, Winston took her hand into his, and she realized what she was about to do before she could manage to muster up enough energy to heal him. Had Sarain not been tired from using so much energy to fight the demon off earlier, she likely would have exposed her secret to Winston, but now with him standing there, holding her hand, and staring down at her longingly, she realized that the injury was far from Winston's mind.

He suddenly pulled her to him, pressing his cold hard body against her soft warm skin. Winston leaned down, taking in a deep breath and inhaling in the scent of Sarain's hair, before finally lowering himself enough so that he could gently kiss her on the lips. Sarain then pulled back for a moment, causing Winston to tense with concern when he noticed that she was studying his fangs. "Do they bother you?" he asked. Sarain silently shook her head "no" as she continued to stare at them, and then she leaned in and began to kiss Winston again, careful to avoid the sharpness of his fangs. The tension in Winston lessened when he realized that Sarain had only been trying to figure out how to kiss him without cutting her lips on his fangs like the previous time they had kissed.

As they kissed, Winston began to move Sarain towards the bed, but once they reached it she stopped, looked up at him, and curiously asked, "Are there any other changes I should be made aware of?" Sarain quickly glanced down and then back up to Winston as she waited for an answer. Winston nearly chuckled as he said, "No, that's all pretty much the same." "Pretty much?" she repeated with a smile as she lay back onto the bed. Winston climbed on the bed next to Sarain, with it heavily creaking, as he reached for her, and began kissing her neck like he always did in the past. He moved his mouth carefully down the nape of her neck, listening to her soft sighs, as he proceeded to kiss down her back. His lips gently moved to her scarred shoulder, and as he began to kiss near her injury, his nose became flooded with the scent of her dried blood. Winston hadn't noticed the smell earlier when he had merely looked at the scrape, but now being so close to it, the scent of her dried blood began to entice him, making him hungry.

In fact, the whole stimulating act began to bring up memories of past lovers that had allowed Winston to feed on them during sex, but that was never the case with Sarain. He began to wonder what her blood might taste like, if it was sweet, and if he would crave it as much as he craved being with her. Winston's eyes began to burn as Sarain shifted around to face him, she wasn't surprised to see his eyes ablaze, since they often became that way when he was aroused. Her hands reached to undo his pants, but as she leaned in towards him, Winston began to find himself fighting a sudden strong urge to bite Sarain. It was unlike any previous urge that he had ever had in the past while in a state of arousal with her; it was almost overpowering. Winston suddenly moved away from Sarain, catching her by surprise.

She stared up at him, her eyes wide with shock, when he began to get up off the bed. Winston abruptly started buttoning up his shirt, and Sarain fretfully questioned, "Did I do something wrong?" "No," he quickly muttered, and then moved towards the door. Sarain grabbed a sheet to cover herself as Winston opened the door, and she called out, "Why are you leaving?" "This…..you and me, it can't happen until you're turned," Winston agitatedly replied. "But I trust that you won't hurt me," Sarain stated. "Well I don't," he told her as he started to step out the room. "Wait, don't go," she pleaded, but it was too late as Winston closed the door shut behind him.

Chapter 31

Hours later, Sarain sat on the bed, redressed, and pondering. She couldn't figure out how to handle Winston. Even after demonstrating her loyalty to him, he still kept his distance from her. Deciding to be with him was proving to be very lonely. She thought of how it should currently be nighttime, though being underground was throwing her senses off to the time of day.

Figuring that Winston was likely awake somewhere in the cavern, Sarain decided that she would go and look for him. A sudden thought popped into her head that she found a little bit comical, it was how she was likely safer at night with the hustle and bustle of many demons awake and moving about the cavern than she was during the day, when a rogue beast could corner her alone.

Sarain got up and headed for the door, and as she pulled the groaning door open, she immediately noticed that standing outside her room weren't the usual scaly demons, but instead were a pair of male vil sangs. She automatically recognized one of the vil sangs as the one that had spoken to her previously, which had made Winston jealous when he had seen them talking.

The familiar vil sang turned to Sarain and remarked, "Ah, you're awake." Sarain gave him a half smile and asked, "Is the king up yet?" "Yes, but... he's out hunting," the vil sang replied, and then added, "But he said that you had his permission to leave the cavern, for the night that is…As long as I accompanied you." "Really?" Sarain asked, surprised. "Yes," he responded, "He actually requested me personally for some reason; he said something about trusting my loyalty to the queen. I thought maybe you had said something to him." Sarain shook her head, and stated, "No, it must have been all you." The vil sang smiled, and said, "Well that's good…Oh, I'm Ethan by the way." She smiled and shook his hand, and then he asked, "So did you want to get out of here?" "Definitely," she quickly replied.

The two walked the long, dark tunnels with Ethan chatting along about his surprise to be singled out for the assignment, and how just the other day most of the vil sangs had been assigned away from the Brotherhood's headquarters. He spoke of how now the vil sangs had all suddenly been recalled back while many of the older demons had been sent away in their place. Sarain nodded her head along as Ethan spoke, but didn't chime in. She suspected why Winston had made such an abrupt and bold move; he no longer trusted the older demons that were likely to still be loyal to Aion. Winston must have figured that the vil sang men would be more prone to be loyal to Sarain, because of seeing her as a woman and not as a threat. Sarain figured that this meant that Winston no longer worried that her eyes would wander to another man; that or he was more worried for her life than her faithfulness.

When they finally reached the entrance to the cavern, Sarain felt a rush of cool night air. It gave her a rejuvenating feeling, and Sarain realized that she missed the night almost as much as she missed the day; she was so sick of being cooped up underground. Ethan turned to Sarain, and asked, "So where did you want to go?" Sarain took a deep breath, thinking for a moment before answering, "I want to go to the mountain's peak." Ethan looked at her curiously, asking, "You don't want to go someplace farther, like in town?" "No, the top of this mountain is where I want to go," she replied. "Ok," he simply said, still appearing to be confused by her choice, but began to lead her safely up the mountainside.

They didn't speak as they trekked up the mountain; Ethan seemed to sense that this was a solemn journey for Sarain. It didn't take long for them to reach the top. Sarain had remembered the journey seeming longer before, but this time the trip felt less ominous. Once they arrived at their destination, Ethan remarked, "Well, here we are," and then gazed around and noted, "It's a nice view up here, you can really see the stars." Sarain nodded, but didn't respond, so the awkward-feeling Ethan added, "With the sky so clear out tonight, it almost looks like you could fall up into it from here." Sarain gave him a puzzled look, thinking of how young Ethan seemed, and wondering how long he had been a vil sang.

"Did you know that I died here?" she suddenly asked him. Ethan's eyes went wide, and he quickly muttered, "No." "I took my father with me, when I died… Did you know Aion?" she inquired. "No, I didn't; I heard some stuff about him, and you, but I'm new at this." "Being a vil sang, you mean?" she asked. "Yeah, I was turned about six months ago, I guess the Brotherhood was trying to increase their numbers, because they turned a lot of us around then," Ethan explained. "I'm sorry," Sarain automatically replied. He looked a little surprised by the remark, but responded by saying, "Thank you." She never asked him if he had chosen the life or not, but she felt that if she were to ask that his answer would be that he hadn't.

Something else lingered in Sarain's mind, and now that they were away from the other demons, she asked Ethan, "Is Winston really out hunting?" He hesitated to respond right away, but eventually he muttered, "He… may be." "Is he avoiding me?" She pressed next. He glanced at her somberly, answering, "…He asked that I keep you away from him until the wedding ritual." "I don't suppose his reason is because of a pre-wedding tradition," Sarain muttered, "Do you know why?" Ethan shook his head "no", and she asked cautiously, "Would you be willing to help me see him?" He stared at her for a moment, as though pondering over the idea before saying, "I'm not sure… He is the King after all." Sarain sighed, stating, "That's okay, I understand."

She gazed up at the sky, the stars twinkling above, and then remarked, "It really is beautiful up here." Sarain then sat down on the ground, and simply stared up at the sky. Ethan took this as a queue that Sarain wasn't looking to go anywhere else, and he sat down on the ground as well. While staring at the stars, Ethan curiously asked, "So how did someone like you get involved with the King?" Sarain smiled, reflecting back while answering,

"Well that's a long story. I guess its best that I start at the beginning…"

It wasn't until near dawn that Ethan and Sarain finally went back into the cavern. He had been enthralled by the story of her life and many adventures, while the relay of his life had been short and, as he deemed, "ordinary until now".

Sarain was exhausted by the time her head hit the pillow, and shortly after she closed her eyes, she heard a light knock against her door. She lifted her head, unsure of if she had actually heard someone knocking, and when it happened again, she got up to answer the door.

Sarain cracked the door open to see that it was Ethan standing on the other side, and he was alone. "Where are the other guards?" she sleepily muttered. "On an errand to bring you fresh food and water, so with that being said, we don't have much time," he hurriedly responded. "Time for what?" she immediately questioned, suddenly becoming more alert. "To get you to Winston's room," Ethan answered. "You know where it is? Are you sure he's there now?" Sarain pried with enthusiasm in her voice. "Yes, I just saw him go into it looking tired," he answered, as he rushed her along, moving quickly down the empty tunnels.

It appeared as though most of the demons were off resting somewhere and the few that they spotted they worked to avoid being seen by. As they neared where Ethan said the room would be, he put a hand up in the air to signal Sarain to stop and peered around the corner.

After the glimpse, he went back to Sarain, leaned to her ear, and whispered, "There are two guards outside his door. It's likely that he told them to keep you away like he told me. I'm going to create a distraction to lure them away, when I do, slip in quickly. There shouldn't be a lock on the door, I think yours is the only room to have one, but if there is, then hurry back to your room and we'll try something else later."

Ethan turned to leave, but Sarain unexpectedly put her hand on his shoulder, and when he glanced back at her to see why, he saw her mouth the words "thank you" to him. He smiled and nodded in return, and then went back to leave so he could make the distraction. Sarain waited at the corner as Ethan walked down the passageway, past the guards, and to the next corridor where, after a minute, a loud noise that sounded like furniture crashing and breaking echoed out. The two demonic guards went rushing to the commotion with Sarain hoping that Ethan was able to keep from being caught. She hurried around the corner once the demons were out of eye sight, racing to the door with the hopes that Winston hadn't had a chance to place a lock on the inside of the door.

Sarain placed her hand on the latch handle of the door, and with a deep breath turned it. The door opened and she slipped into Winston's room. The room was completely black once Sarain closed the door behind her, and it took her several seconds before she was able to make out anything inside the room. But when she could determine where the bed was, in the mass of shadows, Sarain went over to it and climbed onto the large mattress. There she felt for the bulky cold body in the center of the bed, and she curled up next to it, wondering whether or not she should wake Winston. Before she had a chance to make up her mind, Sarain heard his voice say, "What are you doing here, Sarain?" "So you are awake," she muttered. "I have been since I heard that disturbance down the hall, and then I smelt you at the door," he remarked. "Oh… Why didn't you say something sooner?" she asked. "I wanted to see what you were up to; seems like a lot of trouble to sneak in here just to spoon me," Winston stated. "Says you, I think the end justifies the means," Sarain commented as she snuggled up to him.

"Why are you here?" he asked frankly, but not moving away from her either. "I don't want to be kept away from you anymore. I made the worst mistake of my life by leaving you those many years ago; I don't want to waste another moment by being away from you again," she answered wholeheartedly. "It's not safe for me to be around you while you're still mortal, Sarain, I could hurt you," Winston pleaded. "I don't believe that you would, but if it really worries you so much, then let's do this wedding turning ritual thing as soon as we can," she told him. "Really? You're ready to become a vil sang again?" he asked, surprised. "No, but if it means being with you, then I'll do it," she replied.

A tear escaped Winston's eyes, unbeknownst to Sarain. "I only ask that we do this ritual with just you and me; if my mortal life has to end, I only want you there by my side," she appealed to him, "And if you're willing to grant me another request; could we do it just before dawn on the mountain top where I died? I've died and been reborn there once before, it seems fitting for it to happen there again. And I want to see the shades of blue before dawn one last time, if I can never see another sunrise again, at least let me see that." Winston was quiet for a while, before he finally answered, "Of course; just you and me, on top of the mountain, before dawn….We'll do it tonight."

Sarain let out a sigh of relief, but inside she felt scared and anxious. Winston wrapped his arms around her, and they cuddled together, awaiting sleep. Sarain shifted so that she could rest a hand on her stomach as she thought to herself, "Tonight I will tell your daddy about you, baby, and I pray that he'll want to run away with us… I pray he lets me keep you."

Chapter 32

Sarain woke a little before dusk, and to a big empty bed. Winston had apparently woken up before her, and done his best not to disturb her. He had left a single candle burning, so that Sarain wouldn't wake to total darkness. She thought about the conversation they had that morning, and while she feared that Winston would turn her later that night, she was glad that this limbo-like turmoil would soon be over.

Sarain had made her choice in her mind; she wanted to be with Winston, but she also planned to tell him about the baby before he could turn her, in hopes that he would at least delay the turning until their child could be born. Though the nagging worry that Winston might not believe Sarain lingered in the back of her mind, she wondered that if things did go that way, and Winston demanded she be turned now, would she be capable of a least trying to run from him? Sarain doubted her ability to escape Winston's grasp with his demonic speed and power, and she didn't want to have to fight him. Her only real option at that point would be to try and elude him until sunrise, and then she would have no choice but to leave him for the safety of her child. But then, would she come back to him once the baby was born?

Sarain didn't want to think about such things, even if she probably should. Instead, she wondered about what a demonic wedding would be like, aside from the exchanging of blood, like would they exchange vows or rings?

Sarain decided to get up, and get dressed, though all her things were back in her room. So she opened the door and stepped out to see two demons guarding the door, Winston must have told them that she was inside, because they didn't seem surprised to see her. She walked past them, and they didn't follow; she figured that this meant they were ordered to guard the entrance to the room. Sarain made the walk to her room as she remembered it from sneaking around earlier that day. When she turned the corner to the hallway where her room was, she saw that her room also had two guards waiting out in front of it, and was happy to see that one of them was Ethan. She approached him with a smile and said carefully, not to let the other vil sang guarding the door know too much, "I'm glad to see that you're…well." Ethan smiled back, and replied, "Thanks, just another uneventful day for me, nothing to report."

Sarain then opened the door and entered her room where inside she saw candles lit, fresh food and drink waiting for her, and lying on her bed was a simple white dress. As Sarain neared the bed to get a better look at the dress, she saw the glint of something shiny lying on her pillow. She walked over to it to see that her ankh had been cleaned of Kara's flesh, and the broken chain had been replaced. She smiled knowing that Winston had to have been the one to fix it since he was the only demon she knew that was able to touch the ankh without getting burned. She picked up her ankh, and placed it around her neck for what she realized could be the last time; she thought of how she may not be able to wear it for much longer once she was made into a vil sang.

Sarain took a deep breath while looking over at the plate of food, knowing that she should eat, but feeling almost too anxious to do so. Sarain went into the pouch of her backpack, where the old and tattered picture of Orran and her was kept. She placed the photo next to the plate of food, and as she ate, she thought of her old friend and how in a perfect world, he would stand up next to Winston, as his best man, while they recited their vows safely in the light of a perfectly sunny day. It was a dream that Sarain could never see realized, but even still, it was what she wished for.

The hours of the night went by incredibly slow for Sarain, who was mostly kept occupied by Ethan, whom had her relaying more accounts of her battles, and what it was like the first time she had demonic blood coursing through her veins.

As it grew closer to dawn, Sarain got dressed in the soft white dress that went down to her knees while the top was in the style of a camisole. It looked like a spring dress, nothing fancy, but Sarain liked that it lacked girly frills; it was something she would have picked out herself. She left her long dark hair down, and had her ankh still hanging around her neck. The only pair of shoes Sarain had was boots, but they were perfect for her to slip in the picture of Orran and her, so that she could at least have a part of her friend with her for such a life changing moment.

A soft knock came to the door, with Ethan then stepping into the room afterwards, saying, "It's time." But as Sarain moved towards the door, Ethan stopped her by making the comment, "Wait, I have something for you," he then pulled out, from behind his back, a fragile crown made of simple white wildflowers. "I wanted to do something for you, but this is all I could come up with," Ethan said with a hint of disappointment in his voice. Sarain stared at the handmade flower crown, and smiled as it reminded her of the ones she used to make with her mother as a child. "It's perfect," she remarked, nearly tearing up. Ethan's face then lit up and he placed the delicate crown gently on Sarain's head. And with that, he led her out of the room and through the cavern's tunnels.

When they walked through the main corridor, Sarain saw that many of the demons were gathered there, if not all of them. They stared at their soon-to-be Queen, and bowed their heads as she walked by. It was a surreal sight, seeing so many demons looking at her with awe instead of hate; Sarain wasn't sure how it made her feel, but the feeling was definitely a new one. Ethan also appeared to be amazed by the response, not used to seeing the demons so united and honoring a mortal. They continued to walk the corridor, and then went down the tunnel towards the entrance of the cavern.

When they finally stepped outside, Sarain could see that the stars were already fading into the now deep purple night sky. "Looks like we better pick up our pace," Ethan noted, and they headed up the mountainside, as they had done the night before. The wind blew Sarain's hair back and off her shoulders, chilling her skin. She could feel the dread growing inside her, and as if responding to it, she felt her baby flutter around and then kick.

As they neared the mountain's peak, Sarain saw Winston begin to come into view, and her nerves started to calm at the sight of him; he stood there, humbly waiting, wearing a white dress shirt, and black slacks. Though he had his demonic features, to Sarain, Winston simply looked like a man in love; just as any man that has ever been seen waiting at an alter for his bride to come join him. She approached him, serenely, and took one of Winston's clawed hands into hers. Ethan gazed at the couple for a moment, and then said, "Well I got her here on time. I will leave you two to do what you must do," Ethan then glanced at Sarain as he said, with a forced smile, "Good luck."

Winston thanked Ethan before he went, while Sarain realized that the young vil sang was feeling sorry for her; not that she was getting married, but because she was about to be made into something unnatural. Ethan left back down the mountainside, and while still holding Sarain's hand, Winston turned to her and said, "You look beautiful." She smiled, thanked him, and then nervously asked, "Where do we begin?"

Winston gently brought his free hand up to Sarain's cheek, where he caressed back the loose and wind-blown hair off of her face, and then he reached into his pocket and pulled out a small item. He took a hold of Sarain's left hand, brought it up, and then carefully placed a ring onto her ring finger. The ring looked old, and had a gothic style about it; it was a dark silver colored metal with Celtic symbols carved into it, and it had a garnet gemstone being held in place by claw-like prongs. "I've been told that this ring has been with the Brotherhood for centuries. It had been kept on display for years, and apparently, or so I was told, that it has been left waiting for a lost queen to wear it once more," Winston relayed to Sarain. "It fits perfectly," she stated amazed since she saw no flaws in the old carvings that would have been ruined had the ring been resized.

"I don't have a ring for you...," Sarain started to say, but then stopped as she reached for the chain around her neck. She lifted it over her head, and continued to speak again, saying, "But this ankh has always been important to me, and I may not be able to carry it anymore. So I want you to bare it for me." Sarain placed the ankh around Winston's neck, and the pendant rested safely on his chest as though no demon blood tainted him.

Winston's violet eyes began to glow a faint and somewhat peaceful looking light as he smiled down at Sarain, and said, "Sarain, I have been in love with you since the first time I laid eyes on you, even though you were supposed to be my enemy. I have never wanted anything more than to spend my days with you by my side."

Sarain nervously smiled up at him, and she spoke softly and a little shaky as she said, "Winston, I love you more than I have ever thought possible for me to love someone. I love you so much that I came back from the dead and went straight back to you before I could even remember who I was… I don't need an army, power, or even immortality to be happy with you. I just need you; I only want you…and our child."

Winston suddenly flinched, and immediately asked, "What did you just say?" "Our child, your child, is growing inside me," Sarain announced. "That's impossible," he quickly remarked. "I'm sure Aion once thought it was impossible too, but it's true; when I came back as a mortal, I came back more than just whole, Winston, I came back capable of having your child." "No," he insisted again, "You're just trying to stop me from turning you; it's just a clever trick." Sarain felt her nerves begin to fluster with angst, and recalling what her nerves had caused to happen on the way up the mountain earlier, she quickly grabbed Winston's hand and placed it on her stomach. "Sarain this won't convince me that…" he started to say when his eyes went wide at the sudden sensation of little soft kicks against the palm of his hand.

"I'm a few months along, I'll probably start showing soon, and I haven't been with anyone else, it's yours, Winston," Sarain pleaded. "….I believe you," he muttered, "But I don't know what you're asking me to do." "Don't turn me, or at least wait until our child is born! Run away with me if you're willing!" she blurted out. "But the Brotherhood; if we head back inside and you're not turned it will raise up serious flags. And it's too close to dawn to run to anywhere else," Winston exclaimed. "Then we tell them about the baby!" Sarain stated, but Winston immediately replied, "No! I can't trust that one of those beasts won't see you or our child as a threat! No, someone is bound to try to kill you before the baby can be born." "What are suggesting then?" she questioned with confusion. "You need to run, Sarain, you have to leave now, and without me!" he demanded. "No!" she immediately reacted, "I won't leave you behind." "Sarain, what kind of life could we have together with me looking the way I do now, if not with the Brotherhood; I'd have to always stay out of sight, and we could only travel when they'd be out looking for us," Winston tried to reason.

The sky had grown intensely bluer while they had been debating. Sarain began to cry as she pleaded, "I can't leave you again!" Winston stared down at her, his eyes glowing, as he firmly said, "Sarain, if you don't leave now, then I will stand here, and insist on it until I burn! Either way, you'll have to leave without me!" "NO!" she cried back.

Suddenly, a glint off the ankh Winston wore caught Sarain's attention through the blur of tears. Her heart began to race as she glanced over her shoulder and saw that the sun was rising, she then turned back to Winston, in horror, as she saw that his skin was beginning to darken and smoke while he made no attempt to run for shelter. "Winston!" she shouted with fear. "Go!" he urged, but Sarain wouldn't budge. "No, I won't let you kill yourself," she yelled back. "You can't stop me," he simply stated, but that wasn't going to keep Sarain from trying.

She quickly placed her hands on Winston's now hot skin, feeling it crack beneath her fingers. She mustered all her strength to focus her energy, and before long her hands began to glow. Winston stared down at

Sarain, astonished and confused by what he was seeing as he rapidly grew weaker. Winston's skin began to harden, even more than it had been before, but the smoking seemed to slow down. Still, it wasn't enough to save Winston from the sun; he would continue to burn as long as he stayed outside.

"You have to go inside!" she pleaded, but Winston painfully uttered, "No, I can't have you risking your life to come back for me." "WHAT?!" Sarain spoke with shock, realizing that Winston now planned to kill himself whether she left him or not. With a deep breath, Sarain screamed out her frustrations and her agony at the thought of losing Winston, and with that, she shot the last her energy into him.

As she stared up at him, gasping to catch her breath while her own body weakened, Sarain thought of the last thing she could do to save Winston from himself. She quickly took a hold of his hand and brought one of his claws to her wrist. "What are you doing?" he barely was able to ask. Sarain used all her might to drag the sharp claw across her wrist, slicing it open. "NO!" Winston weakly moaned, as he collapsed to his knees, in an effort to struggle to stop Sarain.

Things began to get hazy for Winston, as he fell to the ground completely, with a sudden and deafening pounding drumming through his ears. He felt Sarain forcing his mouth open, and soon after he felt her warm thick blood run over his tongue and down his throat. He glimpsed her tear stained face staring down at him with fear just before everything went white.

Sarain gazed down at the very silent Winston. He had stopped smoking, but he had also stopped moving. Still she held out hope since he had not turned to ash, until, she saw the black blood pooling out from around his eyes, his nose, his ears, and then finally his mouth. "OOOOOOH GOD!" her scream could be heard echoing out. Sarain collapsed on top of Winston's near searing hot body, and she wept harder than she had ever done before. Her body nearly convulsed with her cries, and it took Sarain more than a minute to realize that hers was not the only body shuddering.

She stared down at Winston with astonishment when she realized that his body had twitched, and then she watched as he jerked once more, this time more noticeably. "Winston?" she mumbled with alarm. Winston abruptly and unexpectedly began coughing and gasping for air, Sarain jumped back in surprise, and witnessed as Winston slowly sat up. He groaned and as he moved, his nearly charcoal black skin started to crack and then flake off of his body, exposing the somewhat pink fresh skin beneath it. Sarain reached over to take Winston's hand, and as she did, she felt his claws break away from his fingers. She gasped and stared over at him until Winston finally opened up his eyes and met her gaze, and then her breath caught in her chest.

Sarain gawked at Winston intensely as he gazed back at her with a pair of eyes that were a shade of blue she had never seen on him before. They were a rich hue of blue, but not the vibrant tone that she had remembered: this shade of blue matched the sky, and no light illuminated from them.

A smile spread across Sarain's face as she watched Winston wipe away the old burnt skin off of his body, while the ankh bounced against his new fair skin. He spotted her grin and curiously asked, "What is it?" Sarain continued to smile as she replied, "Can't you feel it? You're mortal again!" The realization suddenly hit him, and Winston gazed up towards the sky to see that the sun was almost completely up, while he remained fine.

Sarain helped Winston to his feet as he continued to stare up at the sky with amazement. After a long moment, he turned to her, and asked, "What happens now?" Sarain took some time to think the question over, before she finally answered, "First, we run from here… And then we give this one a name," she spoke as she placed their hands on her stomach.

The End

Hope you enjoyed the adventure!

Thanks for reading!

Jen Golembiewski

.

www.ingramcontent.com/pod-product-compliance
Lightning Source LLC
Chambersburg PA
CBHW070801200626
46811CB00023B/361